# Lime
## to my
# Coconut

LYNN JOSEPH

# BLACK MERMAID PRESS
BOOKS THAT CHALLENGE THE STATUS QUO

# Chapter One

A large poster of a white sandy beach, crystal blue sea, and red and yellow hibiscus flowers catches my eye.

It more than catches my eye. It hypnotizes me.

"Wow!" I mutter to myself. "I'd give anything to be there right now."

"Me too," a woman standing next to me says.

We lock eyes and nod in solidarity. "I'd move to that damn island tomorrow," she says. "With or without my hubby."

"Me too," I agree wholeheartedly. "With or without my boyfriend."

"Ah!" the woman waves her hand in a dismissive gesture. "If he's just a boyfriend, you can leave him behind. Live your life to the fullest." She grins under her wool hat.

I nod at her sage advice. Then I duck my head because I can hear what's coming out of my mouth and it sounds pathetic.

"I think he's going to propose to me tonight."

"Really?" her eyes open wide. "*Congratulations?!*"

Should I come clean? I don't want to jinx my future.

"Actually, I'm not sure. I *hope* he's going to propose to me tonight."

She puts a hand to her chin. It's the classic, "I'm thinking," sign. "If that's what you want, then I hope he does. But . . ."

She doesn't finish because our subway whooshes into the station with speed and extra wind.

We both push our way forward trying to find space in the overcrowded rush hour train. I can't see her with all the arms stretched above my head. I press my briefcase close to my body and hope I make it to work without anyone coughing on me.

It's the same thing every day. You'd think I'd be used to it by now. But it always feels like an invasion of the body snatchers when those subway doors shut and we hurtle down the dark tunnel from Brooklyn to the East River.

I try my best to hold onto the metal pole. The vision of the tropical beach stays with me like a promise of something good to come.

Chapter Two

I walk into work having survived the commute intact. I work on the forty-second floor of one of New York City's midtown skyscrapers. As I travel up the gold-mirrored elevator, I unwrap my head scarf, neck scarf, and face scarf. I'm the most clothed person in here.

"Black folks don't play with the cold," my mom used to say.

I grew up in upstate New York where it gets colder than this. She still lives there, so apparently we do get used to it.

My assistant greets me with a mocha latte and a bouquet of flowers she must have picked up at the downstairs newsstand because she rarely leaves work. Based on her billable hours, she must sleep on a couch around here.

"Happy birthday, CJ," she chirps.

I stretch out one arm to hug her.

"Thank you, Evelyn. This is so sweet of you. I love them."

She blushes to the tips of her white-blonde hair.

"I cleared your schedule so you can go to the manicurist this afternoon after your lunch with your girlfriends."

We're walking down the hall toward my office. I swing my eyes to her face. "Why do I have to go to the manicurist?"

"Ahem!" She clears her throat and eyes my left hand clutching the mocha latte. "For your . . . you know what tonight."

I frown. "How do you know about that?"

She scrunches her eyes at me. "I know everything about you. That's my job."

"Oh, okay," I say, though I am sure she got her intel from Giselle, who has the biggest mouth of all my friends. "Thank you."

She nods and then swings open my office door dramatically. "Ta-da!"

My desk and chair are hidden behind an obscenely large vase of delicate pink roses with an overpowering fragrance.

"Wow!" I'm almost afraid to step inside and get swallowed by the ginormous arrangement.

"Happy birthday from Marcus O'Brien," Evelyn says. "You're so lucky," she adds. "I would die to have a boyfriend who'd send me something so beautiful for my birthday."

I nod numbly.

"Anyway," Evelyn claps her hands. "You have two back-to-back client meetings this morning. After that, you are free for the rest of the day."

"Who's first?"

She checks her iPad. "The in-house counsel for the cruise ship that wrecked on that atoll in the South Pacific. The passengers were stranded on board for days before relief came. They're suing for negligence etc., etc. It's a maritime case."

I screw up my face. "Seriously, they got a few extra days on a cruise ship and they're complaining?"

Evelyn nods. "Apparently they felt trapped."

"Some people just like to complain."

I grab my briefcase and beeline toward the conference room to meet my first client.

The rest of the day passes in a blur. Mostly because by noon I have already had three glasses of champagne accompanied by only a few crackers with caviar.

After lunch, it's the manicurist where I choose a pale pink color for my nails that would look beautiful with any kind of stone.

All day long my mother sends text messages. My father sends a virtual card with a note that one of his art pieces will be shipped to my home. I send my thanks and offer to pay for shipping.

Finally, it's six o'clock. I head downstairs to race home and get dressed for dinner. Marcus has texted that he's in the city and will send a car to pick me up at eight. My tonsils are beating with excitement against the back of my throat.

"Yes, mama," I talk to myself as I bathe and dress. "You will soon be engaged to Marcus O'Brien. You will be officially off the market. And so will he. Tomorrow when you wake up next to him, you will start planning your wedding!"

A shiver of excitement races through every bone in my body.

"I'm getting married. I'm getting married." A mantra has taken up residence in my eardrums.

I brush my teeth, giving them a quick polish so they are glittering white against my dark skin. I apply my makeup in slow meticulous strokes.

I must look perfect tonight. It's a once-in-a-lifetime experience. Isn't that what Marcus said on the phone.

"I'm getting married. I'm getting married." The mantra hums on.

"Be quiet," I say out loud to the mirror. "You'll jinx me."

But I don't believe in signs or superstitions. I believe in working hard toward your goals and focusing until you achieve them.

Now that I've accomplished most of my career goals, it's time I turn toward my personal ones. Marrying Marcus is the next logical step in my life plan. On paper, everything lines up.

When the town car arrives, I'm waiting downstairs. My heart flutters at seeing Marcus again after a month apart. His international businesses require him to travel often.

The driver opens the back door. The wide empty back seat greets me like a cold shoulder.

"Mr. O'Brien will be at the restaurant," the driver says as if reading my mind.

I nod. I thought he'd leap out, grab me up, and spin me around. Like they do in the movies. And in all the romance novels I barely have time to read.

I shake my head to erase my foolish, girly fantasies.

Still.

The sight of the dark, empty seat makes my doubts resurface. Even though I am headed to the most important dinner of my life, I can't help but wonder, are Marcus and I honestly soulmates?

<h1 style="text-align:center">Chapter Three</h1>

Marcus O'Brien is larger than life both in person and in the media. His name is well-known. His face, even more so. When I met him five years ago, he was already rich. Now he's on the verge of ascending to the big money playing field. The billionaire stratosphere.

He was, and still is, intensely focused on building his

empire. After a few dates, he told me he needed a strong Black woman by his side.

I was honored he chose me.

"Strong Black woman" is a badge I wear proudly. But do I really want that to be the reason he loves me? What about my sexual side that wants to try new things? My mushy side that loves country western songs and reads romance books, highlighting the swoon-worthy sections and re-reading them when I'm feeling lonely.

Not lonely. I have a man. How can I feel lonely?

All my doubts and questions vanish when I walk into the restaurant and see Marcus's tall, broad-shouldered figure in a suit and tie of such elegance you know it's tailor-made. Even the tie.

He rises from his brocaded armchair. The table is exquisitely set for two. Floor-to-ceiling windows reveal the twinkling lights of New York City.

"Wow!" I murmur, as I press my cheek to his.

He doesn't like to kiss me when I'm wearing lipstick, so we've perfected this cheek-to-cheek greeting in public.

His dark eyes flicker over me and he nods approvingly at my haute couture Dior dress. I'm a princess at a ball. He steps in front of the server and pulls out my chair himself.

I slide in as demurely as possible. My beautiful floaty dress feels like it may slide off my shoulders if I don't maintain a stiff posture for the entire evening.

"Happy birthday again," Marcus says as he sits across from me.

I look around, almost expecting to see balloons and ribbons and a big forty on a hanging decoration. But that's not Marcus. He's classy and low-key. Why would I imagine that scenario?

You'd never know Marcus is from the Bronx. He speaks like

he went to Oxford, dresses like Lucifer Morningstar, and has the focus and leadership skills of a top chef.

The server flicks open the brocaded napkin and rests it on my lap so gently it feels like it's invisible.

"Thanks," I whisper to the tall, perfectly postured man at my side. I could take lessons from him.

"You look lovely," says Marcus.

"Thanks," I smile at my soon-to-be fiancé. I forget my dress and lean forward to hold Marcus's hands. "I missed you."

He leans back with a sparkling smile. "Same."

It doesn't escape me that he slides his hands out of mine. But then I see he is reaching for something in his jacket pocket.

Oh my God! He's not waiting for our meal. He's going to ask right now.

I need to stall him. I need time to set up my phone so I can videotape this epic, once-in-a-lifetime proposal.

I promised my girlfriends I'd do so. Well, that was after a few glasses of bubbly when doing so seemed reasonable.

But how would it look now if I pulled out my iPhone and propped it against the crystal vase of lilies in the middle of the table?

"How was your flight home?" I ask to stall him. My heart thumps with excitement and . . . something else.

His hand stops moving toward his jacket pocket. "Long."

"Oh, right. Anything interesting happen on your flight?"

"No." He frowns. Starts reaching again.

Marcus does not do idle conversation. No small talk. No chit-chats. No fun, flirty dialogues. To Marcus, words are only of value if they are accomplishing something specific.

My mind flies in a hundred directions trying to think of something to say that would be valuable to him.

"How's your stock doing?" I tilt my face in a hopefully sexy manner as I reach into my beaded purse under the table to extract my phone.

His eyebrows dip down into a V. "Which one?"

"Um . . . the *new* one?"

God, I sound like an idiot. My phone's strap catches on the silk lining of the purse. Good God, for real? Must I rip my new purse to get it out?

"What are you doing, Carmela?"

"It's CJ, remember?" I say as I yank hard on my phone.

Oh no, I sound annoyed. I smile to make up for it.

"It's just that Carmela reminds me of my mother. Like I'm about to be schooled."

"Your mother *is* a teacher. And Carmela is a noteworthy name."

"Hmmm." I wonder if I'll have to start calling myself Carmela O'Brien. Once we're married. It does sound better than the option. CO instead of CJ. I stifle a laugh.

The server brings over the famous dark bottle with a gold cap. My favorite champagne. Best in the world.

"Yes, please." I practically stick my glass under the server's nose as he pops the cork.

Am I losing my mind here? Focus CJ. I look at the light brown face and slanted dark eyes of the man sitting across from me.

He's just a man. Asking the woman he loves to marry him.

While the server pours out the delicious sparkling liquid into our flutes, I manage to slide my phone out. I prop it next to the flowers. I've already turned on the video. I make sure Marcus doesn't see it.

I'm recording every amazing moment to share with my girls. And to look at later in life on anniversaries.

Marcus will be glad I thought of this.

I glance at the menu, so I'll be ready to order. Marcus doesn't like it if I ask questions about the dishes. He says, we're at the best restaurants so we should trust the chef to know what he or she is doing.

I think that takes all the fun out of dining. Interacting with waiters is the reason to eat out. Who doesn't want to query them about what dishes they like? Which fish is the preferred one? And are the desserts made in-house?

Marcus calls that idle chit-chat.

I sigh to myself. I want to ask the server about this pheasant dish. I'd like to try something new. But what if I don't like it?

"You ready to order?" Marcus asks.

I nod and tell the server I'll take the salmon. With Marcus, it's better to go the safe route. No time to waste. No space to experiment.

When he's not working, he wants a simple life. I guess that means I'm simple. I do try to be easygoing, no trouble, amenable.

I'm about to take a much-needed sip of my champagne.

He raises a hand. "A toast is appropriate for this occasion."

I lower my glass, my heart pounding in anticipation.

"Yes?" I hope I look chill. Not like a woman jonesing for a ring. No pun intended.

"Ms. Carmela Jones," he starts.

I almost roll my eyes at the way he stresses the word, "Carmela." Fortunately, I catch myself. I rearrange my face into a look of sweet serenity.

"Yes, Mr. O'Brien?"

His smile could charm the cows upstate. "It's been a wonderful five years together. I am happy I get to be your ride-or-die. I want to present you with a gift that shows my deep commitment to you."

I can't help it. A burp erupts from my throat. The bubbles in my champagne must be playing havoc with my nerves.

"Sorry," I murmur. Rocket fuel suffuses my face.

Another deep V mars his beautiful forehead. "Are you okay?"

I nod, afraid to open my mouth in case another burp escapes. I glance at my phone. I hope the video is still running. This is taking a lot longer than expected.

"Right." He drums his manicured fingers on the table. "Anyway, you know your value. I want to reward it."

*Reward*? An alarm bell triggers in my head. What the hell is he talking about—*reward*?

His hand grabs something from inside his jacket's breast pocket.

Oh my God.

I can't look.

My heart races like a jackrabbit under a full moon.

I close my eyes, squeezing my lids down tightly.

I press my fingers to my lips, so I don't burst out crying. Marcus hates scenes.

"Are you going to look at your present?"

His voice sounds so . . . detached.

My eyelids spring open. My hands drop to my lap. Sitting on the table is a plain white envelope.

A *flat* envelope.

What the hell?

"Open it," he smiles, full of confidence.

Part of me is wondering how this envelope leads to the actual down on one knee, offering a ring box, will you marry me scene.

"Okay," I say fake cheerfully. I can play along. I rip open the envelope.

Two pieces of paper flutter out. My heart hitches.

"*Welcome to St. Nicholas's Cocoa Reef Resort*" is written on the top of both pieces of paper.

Destination wedding, maybe?

I look up quizzically.

"It's the bucket list holiday you told me you dreamed of. You put up pictures of the island of St. Nick all over your vision board last year, remember?"

I nod stiffly.

"I took off from work. We are going there next week. You know I don't take vacations. But I want to show you how much you mean to me."

Traitorous tears form in the backs of my eyes.

Don't you dare cry.

Marcus hands me another envelope. "Here's our tickets and our premium reservation at the resort. Everything is planned. A boat trip. An island hike. Even a couples massage."

I smile as best as I can, staring down at the thin slips of paper. They're almost invisible. As invisible as the ring I imagined I'd be getting tonight.

The server appears with the first course. He places a crystal bowl of the most beautiful salad with edible flowers in front of my face. The flowers have delicate drops of water trembling on their petals. A few more drops won't be noticeable.

"Well? Are you excited?"

My shoulders must be drooping because my dress straps have slid down so far, it's like I'm wearing a strapless gown.

Try as I might, I cannot form the right words to say thank you. It's a great gift. It's the kind of gift I should be thrilled to receive. But it means nothing right now.

I lift my head and lock eyes with Marcus.

He leans back in his chair, folds his arms across his chest. "What?" he asks.

I see it clearly. The wall of defense he erects when I confront him about anything he does not want to talk about.

I don't know where I find the strength to do it, but I open my mouth and say clearly. "Are you ever going to ask me to marry you, Marcus O'Brien?"

I do not blink.

Neither does he.

I can see why this man is a top-tier businessman.

But I am a first-class litigator. I face judges and juries. I confront opposing counsels and defiant witnesses. I cross-examine people for a living!

How can I forget all that when I'm with this man? A man who has taken *five years* to finally decide . . . that he can go on vacation with me.

Hot blood boils in my veins.

"It's a yes or no question, Mr. O'Brien."

"Then, no. Not right now."

"Thank you." I stand up, slip my dress straps up my arms, and grab my flute of champagne. I tip it to my mouth, drinking every delicious drop then refilling my glass and doing it again.

"You are making a scene. Sit down."

I laugh. "So what? By the way, full disclosure. I recorded us." I pick up the phone and point it at him.

I slide the phone into my purse, then pick up the envelope with the tickets and reservations. "And I'll be using this birthday present. Thank you very much. Just not with you. I'm done."

At this, he stands up. "You're breaking up with *me*?"

I run my eyes up and down his handsome face and powerful body. I shake my head. "Can you believe how long it took me to do it? They say you gain wisdom with age. I guess I finally got old enough."

I didn't mean for it to come out so hostile. It makes me

wonder if I've been holding onto some latent anger towards him. Anger that is now bubbling over.

With my purse on my shoulder, the envelope tucked under one arm, I reach for the half-full Dom Perignon bottle. "I'll take this too. Goodbye, Marcus."

# Chapter Four

Have you ever been in the middle of doing something that your heart urges, but your mind is in the background yelling, "Stop! Halt! Slow your roll!?"

As I storm out of the fancy sky-high restaurant and ride the elevator down to the lobby, I feel more than champagne gurgling inside my stomach. I feel an entire acid rainstorm brewing.

What did you just do? You broke up with your boyfriend who bought you an epic birthday gift because it wasn't a ring?

Seriously CJ?

Since when are you a prima donna?

I hang my head. I can't look at the woman in the gilded mirrors adorning the interior of the elevator.

I can't go running back to him. I can't apologize.

Not when my heart is saying, "You did the right thing."

I did do the right thing, I tell my reflection. Now live with it.

But that was not how my mother saw it the next day.

"Are you out of your mind, Carmela Jones? Some men take longer to commit. Did Marcus do anything to cause this breakup? Did he cheat? Did he lie? Did he hit you? Huh?"

"Mom," I whisper. "I'm at work." Although truthfully, I'm not getting any work done on this cruise ship case. Or on any case. My brain is so far from the office, it's already on vacation.

Giselle, Lisa, Mikah, and Katana hit me up on a video conference call and I say goodbye to Mom. We've been a friend group since we all met at Howard University over twenty years ago. Sometimes, we forget we're not eighteen anymore. We forget we're grown-ass women with careers and our own money.

"Well!" they shout. "Show us the ring."

I hate disappointing my girls. But I have no choice.

"There's no ring. But I do have an extra ticket to an all-expense paid vacation to the island of St. Nick." I wave the flimsy pieces of paper in the air so they can see. "My birthday present."

"What?" they echo each other. "No ring?"

I swivel around in my office chair.

"Tell all, please," Lisa says. "Don't leave out any details." Lisa is an astrophysicist. I kid you not. She takes the expression "beauty *and* brains" to a whole new level.

I give them the whole truth. Leaving out nothing to save face. It is what it is.

They listen in silence. No interruptions, and no comments from the peanut gallery. When I'm done, I see looks on their faces I did not expect.

Smiles of happiness. Even relief.

"Why are you all looking so happy?" I frown. "I just broke up with my man of five years. A good man. For literally no reason."

"Oh CJ, we never wanted you to marry Marcus. You act so differently around him. All meek and quiet and accommodating," Giselle says.

Giselle has known me the longest since we met at Freshman Orientation. So she would know.

"Yes, we have nothing against Marcus. But he doesn't bring out your true self," Katana remarks.

"Exactly," Lisa says. "It's like you turn into a version of yourself you think he'd approve of. Instead of the woman we know and love with all your bitchy ways."

"I do nothing of the sort," I hiss.

"Find a man who can appreciate your flaws and imperfections as well as your incredibly loyal, loving side," Giselle says soothingly.

"You guys waited five years to tell me Marcus is not the right man for me?" I huff. "Thanks a lot. Just for that, I'm not taking any of you with me on this trip."

"Good," Mikah says. "Because you should go alone and spend time with yourself."

Easy for her to say. Mikah is a model and is used to traveling by herself to international destinations for runway shows. Even close to forty, her bone structure is still killing it.

"I was kidding," I interrupt her spiel. "I don't want to go alone."

Silence on the other end.

"Look, CJ," Giselle says. "The reason no one told you Marcus wasn't the right man is because every time we tried, you'd come back with how smart he is, how much money he makes, how lucky you are. It's time you went off by yourself and rediscovered who *you* are. How lucky any man would be to have *you* in his life."

I sniff. "Lisa just called me a bitch."

Lisa laughs. "I said *bitchy ways*. Which you do have. As do we all."

"Like what?" I grumble.

"Like how you're always complaining about the weather, the subway, the noise in the condos near yours, the way the mailman leaves your mail in an untidy mess, the way the local bodega doesn't carry your favorite bagels. You need more examples?"

"I'm just trying to live an optimum experience."

"Right," Katana laughs, rubbing her huge belly. "Try doing so with a human inside you growing into a giant basketball."

I catch sight of Katana's strained face. She's married to a wonderful man we all vetted, and now they have 1.5 kids.

"I'm sorry. I don't mean to be so . . ."

"Self-centered?" asks Mikah.

Everyone laughs. "I was going for 'ungrateful.'"

"What are you going to do when he calls and tries to talk you into getting back together?" Mikah asks.

"He won't. He was in shock that I'd break up with *him*."

"I suppose that would come as a shock to any billionaire."

"But he's a man first," I say. "And as a man, he didn't live up to my needs."

"Just remember that when he comes crawling back to you."

"If there's one thing I know for sure. It's that Marcus O'Brien is not the 'crawling back to anyone' type."

# Chapter Five

Two weeks later, I'm standing in the middle of the luxurious lobby of the Cocoa Reef Resort with a pretty straw hat in one hand and a rum punch with a lime twist in the other. I'd just arrived and hadn't even gotten my room key when the cocktail was placed in my hand by a welcoming committee.

"This is delicious," I exclaim truthfully.

I hold it up and look at the bottom of the glass as if expecting to see some magic words written there. In the last two weeks I've moped around, cried myself to sleep, and argued with my mother. This cocktail is the first thing that has brought a smile to my face since the epic breakup.

It was even in the news. Someone in the restaurant had captured me storming out with the bottle of champagne and it was all over social media before the end of the night.

Headlines read, "The new billionaire is on the market." And "Meet NYC's most eligible bachelor."

I had to get away. I couldn't take the pitiful looks from everyone in the office. Or the demands from TMZ reporters trying to confirm the rumors. Or worse, my mother calling every hour to find out if a) I wanted to come upstate, or b) wanted her to come to me.

"Glad you like it. It's a specialty of our supreme mixologist, Keston Kips. You can get as many as you like from the beach bar during the day and the pool bar at night."

"Sounds like Keston Kips is the man to meet," I joke ruefully.

"He *is* our most popular employee for good reason."

Great. Another man with a following.

I push thoughts of New York and Marcus out of my head and focus on my surroundings. Balmy tropical air. Fragrant flowering bushes all around. The sound of waves hitting the sand in the distance.

I inhale deeply and let it out.

"When is Mr. O'Brien arriving?" the receptionist interrupts my impromptu meditation.

"He isn't. He couldn't make the trip. It'll just be me."

"Oh, I'm sorry to hear he won't be joining us."

"Me too," I mutter softly.

"Well," the woman smiles. "We will make sure you enjoy your time with us. There are many activities at Cocoa Reef."

"Thanks. I came for the peace and quiet. I'd really prefer to be left alone if you don't mind. I don't want to participate in any activities."

"That's fine, too," she pivots smoothly. "Many guests seek the calming atmosphere we are known for. I will make sure you are not disturbed. You are free to not speak to anyone if you choose. We have had guests who take vows of silence while they are here."

"Really?" My eyebrows shoot up as I consider if I want to try that.

"No, that's okay. But maybe you can get my mother to take that vow."

She laughs with me.

The next thing I know I'm being whisked off in a golf cart to a private villa that I have all to myself.

Set amidst a garden blooming with tropical flowers are two coconut trees flanking the patio large enough to play handball in. I'm dazed at the beauty and affluence.

Marcus booked us a fricking *palace*.

The interior is all marble, glass, and giant ceramic vases overflowing with fresh flowers in case I get tired of the planted ones outside.

Home for the next two weeks!

I spin around. It almost makes me forget I'm grieving the loss of a five-year relationship.

Five years is a long time. You get used to certain things. Like nightly phone calls. Early morning text messages. And someone besides your mother asking how you feel.

I walk into the massive bedroom. A king-sized bed sits on a platform. The sparkling white duvet is covered with pink rose petals.

My eyes fall on the silver bucket of ice next to the bed. The gold wrapper on the bottle reveals the ultimate Dom Perignon champagne. Tears fill my eyes remembering the last time I held a similar bottle.

Marcus thought of everything.

Well, his assistant more likely, but still.

I sink down on the bed, pushing aside petals so I don't crush them.

*Did I make a big mistake? Was I too hasty?*

Tears prick the corners of my eyes. The funny thing is I have not cried at all. As if I'm still in shock from the breakup. Or in shock he said marriage wasn't on his radar. How could I be so clueless?

Now, staring at the champagne that I can't pop open by myself, and the beautiful bed perfect for romantic nights, I feel ill. As if I've turned a page in my book and there's nothing but a blank one staring back at me.

## Chapter Six

**E**nough! I scowl at my mournful face in the mirror.

You're on vacation. On the epic St. Nicholas Caribbean island. Where luxury meets nature. *Pull up your big girl panties and get outside.*

I force myself to get up off the deliciously comfy bed, where I long to sink beneath the duvet and cry my eyes out.

I unzip my new luggage and pull out the last thing I packed. A brand new, teeny tiny, two-piece swimsuit in the brightest yellow I've ever seen. It instantly takes me back to the scene last night at my condo in Brooklyn.

"I'll be a walking neon sign," I exclaimed to my girls when I unwrapped the flimsy pieces of cloth.

Giselle, Mikah, and Lisa had come over to celebrate my birthday belatedly bearing gifts. Katana joined us via video call.

I was in no mood to celebrate anything for a week after my actual birthday, so they were making it up to me before my trip.

My gifts had a theme. Sexy beachwear. Including several crocheted coverups, one of which looks like it costs a small nation its entire GNP.

White feathery mules that make my legs look long and lean and scream, "Fuck me now."

I had tossed them aside, but Lisa tucked them into my suit-case. "Nope, you're wearing these suckers. In or out of bed. But wear them."

I sighed. "This is a trip to meditate on new goals. Now that I'm forty I don't have time to waste. I need to focus."

"Woman, you've done nothing but focus since you came out of the womb. Please enjoy some BDE with an island hottie. For us." Katana swooned on the screen, clasping her hands to her chest.

"Right!" Giselle added. "Find you a hot sexy island man and get back on your horse."

I rolled my eyes.

"I heard they have BDE like crazy down there," Katana sighed.

"I'm almost afraid to ask." I held up a palm. "BDE means .. .?"

Before I even finished, they all shouted, "Big dick energy! Girl, where've you been?"

"I refuse to be shamed for not knowing what BDE is."

Katana shouted, "Even I know it and love it."

We all shook our heads at her. "You can't even get up without help and you're talking about the thing that made you this way." Lisa choked on a laugh.

Katana stuck out her lip. "Just get some. But with a condom."

I wish I could laugh thinking about my friends. But their pressure for me to sleep with a new man so soon is a bit much.

The most I could promise them was that I'd wear the sexy outfits.

"Outside! You have to wear them *outside* your room," Lisa said.

"We know you lawyers *love* your loopholes," said Mikah.

I'd laughed along with them. Not a hearty, belly laugh like they were doing. But a small, *I'll give it my best-shot* laugh.

Something between a hope and a promise.

<h1 style="text-align:center">Chapter Seven</h1>

Dressed in an obscenely sparkly silver beach dress, feathery mules on my smartly pedicured toes, and a wide-brimmed straw hat on my head, I venture outside.

"Do your worst," I tell the towering coconut trees as they wave their leafy branches at the shell-pink evening sky.

I'm not letting my all-inclusive premium drink package go to waste.

I slide into the golf cart that I have exclusive use of for the entire vacation. I've never driven one, so I check out the pedals, the steering wheel, the canopy.

Then, *vroom, vroom.*

Okay, it's no Formula One race car. But it gathers its muscles, and we rumble off down the path. I drive toward the sound of gentle waves breaking on the shore.

I get as far as the beach bar. It's an authentic large wood and palm-leaf tiki hut. A banyan tree grows in the middle, poking up through the tightly woven wooden rafters. Bar stools made of heavy wood in a wide array of colors circle tall barrel tables. Skull and bone flags flutter from the roof beams. Shockingly white sand *is* the floor, making the "sand between your toes" vibe a reality.

Hammocks are strung between trees.

It looks like a set design from Disney's *Pirates of the Caribbean.* The only thing missing is Captain Jack Sparrow clutching a bottle of rum.

Before I can climb out of the golf cart, a handsome young man hurries over to my side.

With a dazzling smile, he offers me his arm.

"Thank you," I remember to smile back. Although his assistance makes me feel a bit aged.

He leads me to one of the empty barrel tables. Up close, I realize it's a real barrel, probably from holding real rum years ago. After telling him I would like to try another one of the famous rum punches, his face lights up even more than it was before.

"Ah! You want a KK?"

"A what?"

"A Keston Kips. That's the name of the bartender who

turned our regular rum punch into something everyone can't get enough of with his secret ingredient. No one can figure it out."

I scrunch up my nose. "No one?"

The young man, whose nametag reads, "Dex," points to a blackboard sitting in the sand next to the bar. "Oh, you can try. Like the rest of the guests. The winner gets a prize. Don't ask me what it is because no one has ever won."

I squint at the list of names and the possible secret ingredients.

"Okay, I'll try. After I drink another one."

Dex turns to go.

"Wait," I touch his arm. "Where is this famous Keston Kips?" I peer over to the bar. A young woman is blending what looks like piña coladas.

Dex jerks a thumb behind me. "At the beach."

"Oh," I glance at the water, which is only a few hundred yards away. The Caribbean Sea encircles this tiny island. I'm not surprised that the water is a majestic blue, kicking off white foam as it kisses the sand.

It's deserted right now. No one in sight.

Dex waves his hands. "He's around somewhere."

I shake my head. Clearly, Keston Kips is a beach bum with a talent for mixing drinks for tourists and then disappearing.

But there is no denying it. He has talent.

As I wait for my rum punch to show up, I look around at the other guests. Almost all are coupled up. Except for a table with four women who look like they're on a girls' trip.

Not one single person is by themselves like me.

I straighten my shoulders. So what?

Dex drops off my punch on his way to another table with a tray full of pretty cocktails.

I stir the cinnamon stick and sip the tangy, savory potion. Hmmm . . . I have no idea what is in this other than rum.

I sniff the drink to see if I can detect the secret ingredient, but no luck.

Screw it. I gulp the delicious cold cocktail and wave to Dex for another.

My girls would be proud of me. I'm going to enjoy every bit of this adventure. Starting with Keston Kips' famous blend.

With the sunset tinging the sky a golden orange, and soulful reggae blasting on speakers nestled high under coconut branches, I swing around in my bar stool to capture the glorious view with my phone's camera.

I even take a couple of selfies with the sinking sun until Dex insists on taking my phone and snapping a few of me as I fake cheer with my rum punch glass.

"Another one, Miss?"

I shake my head no and swill down the last dregs of what is the best drink of my life. Not counting the other two I've already devoured.

Normally I'd stop at two. But envy at seeing all the couples in love, leaning toward each other, or holding hands across the tables, is working its way through me like a virus. I want to forget who should be sitting with me right now. Forget him completely. And these KK specials, as good as they are, are not magic.

I fiddle with the cute pink umbrellas and tiny plastic swords, spearing slices of lime that I've taken out of the rum drinks and lined up on a napkin.

"He sure knows how to make a drink," I slur at poor Dex as he brings me a bottle of water without me even asking.

"That he does, Miss. That he does."

"Yup." A loud hiccup escapes. I slap a hand over my mouth. "Sorry."

Dex smiles. "Keston calls his rum punch the best truth serum. Whatever you feel or think or say under its influence is the truth."

"I'll have to remember that." I wobble off the beach stool. "Time to check out the beach."

"There's a beach wedding going on that way," says Dex, pointing. "Maybe you'll find Keston over there helping. Or you could just enjoy the sunset ceremony. People come from all over the world to get married here."

"Is that right?" I squeeze my eyes shut tightly. Another hiccup breaks through my defenses. I sound like I'm gasping for breath.

"You okay, Miss?"

I grab my water bottle in one hand as I kick off my mules. No need to go falling over on my first day. Although truth be told, these drinks are worth falling over for. I laugh sadly at Dex. "I will be." *Hiccup!*

I wonder what Marcus would say if he could see me now.

# Chapter Eight

I do not recommend trying to walk across soft sand while under the influence. For one, it's tiring. Each footstep feels like my foot is sinking into a sand trap. It's a complete workout of my calf muscles to raise them up and out and move forward.

And two, this short sparkly dress isn't helping. Every couple of steps I take, I have to unwedge the tiny piece of material sliding between my butt crack.

I can't look too pretty, waddling and yanking and waddling again. Like a penguin with hemorrhoids.

"Finally!" I sigh, having reached the top of a mound of sand and wavy beach grass. A bunch of trees shelters the spot from the sun during the daytime I imagine.

I'm ready to collapse on the grass to take in the wedding ceremony below.

It hasn't started yet, going by the fact there is no bride in sight.

People are milling about kissing, hugging, and greeting each other like long-lost relatives, which I suppose they are.

I suddenly wish I was clutching another of Keston Kips' notorious truth serum rum punches instead of this innocuous water.

"But who would I confess my truth to?" I ask aloud. I gaze at the sky where dark birds with long tails frolic and dive toward the sea like kamikaze pilots.

"You all are not helping."

"And what is my truth anyway?" I speak to the birds. "That I dumped my billionaire boyfriend and stole his tickets to paradise? And now I'm sitting on a beach watching a wedding I will never have?"

A nearby cough catches my attention.

"Who's there?" I peer into the distance. The red glowing sky is reflecting onto the smooth ripple-free sea.

At some point without realizing it, I sat down on the seagrass. My legs stretch out in front of me. My bare toes wiggle in the balmy air. My silver dress catches the rising moonlight and sparkles even more.

"Is anyone there?" I ask again.

I hitch up the strap of my dress. My girls said this was beachwear. It's not living up to its name or purpose.

"Hello?" A growing fear makes me hiccup loudly. I don't say excuse me. What's the point? Either a murderer is taking me down or someone is messing with me.

"Maybe you should drink some of your water." The concerned voice is sing-song deep. A cross between a unicorn's magic and a lion's growl.

"Maybe you should mind your business."

In my head, I'm going, *"Whoa! CJ? Why so hostile?"*

But I already know why. I'm officially *off* men telling me what to do.

"Show yourself," I demand in a queenly voice, sucking up any traitorous hiccups.

At that moment, out from the shadows of a sprawling tree steps a large dark figure.

In a tux.

He's at least six feet, with brown skin that's not just brown, it's burnished like a living color that shifts with his movements.

His hair is curly and clipped but also inviting. Like it would be enjoyable to run my fingers through his waves.

*Shut up, CJ. Don't even go there.*

He walks toward me. I hold my breath.

Damn, those shoulders are bigger than Marcus's. Those hips are leaner. That jaw is more chiseled. He's a walking Ken doll on the beach.

Literally.

A giggle escapes.

"You are easily amused," he says in that sing-song voice that I could listen to all day.

I can't stop staring. It must be those rum punches. Makes it hard to put up a façade of indifference.

"**A**re you the groom?" I finally blurt out.

He shakes his head. "No."

"Thank God," I breathe out.

"What? I missed that."

"Oh nothing," I mutter. "I was thanking God you aren't a serial killer."

A deep chuckle erupts from his chest. "I appreciate not being taken for a serial killer."

My heart is racing but I don't know if it's because I'm alone in a strange place at night . . . being from New York I should know better . . . or because the man has an incredibly sexy smile sliding up the corners of his mouth.

"It must be the tux. Makes me look presentable every time." He pretends to dust fake lint off his lapels.

How can a man be so incredibly handsome and give off such playful vibes at the same time?

In my experience, men as handsome as this dude are arrogant. They rely on their looks for their power. They are exceedingly dismissive.

Not. This. Man.

He reaches my side and sticks out a hand to help me up.

"I'm good down here," I say. Mostly because I'm afraid once he hauls me up, I won't be able to stay up.

"Those rum punches catch up with you, don't they?" I say, offering my first smile as if it's a prize. "I presume you've tried them. It's the first thing they give you once you arrive here. Which I just did."

*Ramble much, CJ?*

He clasps his hands in front of his body. "I have tried them. You must be careful."

"Right. They need to put up a sign at the bar."

His lips expand into a wide smile. His teeth are white and sparkling. Ken doll vibes intact.

"So, you're in the wedding party?" I ask, flicking a hand in the direction of the beautiful scene below. Brown paper bag lanterns have been lit all along the rose petal-strewn pathway to the arched canopy of flowers.

"It's so pretty," I sigh. Tears dare to fall but I choke them away.

"Yes."

"Friend of the bride or the groom?"

"Both," he says. "I introduced them."

I look up at him. "Good for you. For them. How lucky they are to have you as a friend."

"Thanks. It's what I do."

"What is what you do?"

He shrugs those beefy shoulders. "I'm basically a therapist. I helped them figure out their issues so they could focus on their love."

I sit up straighter. "You're a therapist?"

He shrugs again. "Basically."

"Where's your office?" I'm ready to sign up for sessions.

That sexy smile makes its way slowly across his face. "I work at the resort."

I blink at him. I knew the resort was all-inclusive. But I didn't know it offered in-house therapy sessions.

Although, why not? What do people need the most on their vacations? Besides a good spa.

"That's amazing," I say. Part of me is wondering how in the world a man this sexy and smooth could be a therapist. But that's beauty discrimination, right?

I'm disqualifying his expertise because he's good-looking. I hated when people told me, "You're too pretty to be a lawyer." Like what the hell?

He nods. "I couldn't help but hear you before. I'm sorry you're having relationship problems."

"You have no idea. I came here to get myself sorted out."

"Well, the wedding doesn't start for another half hour if you want to get anything off your chest. I'm all ears."

"Right here?"

"If you want."

"Oh my God, where should I start?"

"The beginning is always good. But I should tell you, I'm not a . . ."

I don't hear the rest of what he's saying. I'm too busy figuring out whether to start at the elevator ride meet cute with Marcus, or skip all of that and go to the date where Marcus said he wanted a strong Black woman by his side and I thought he meant *as a wife*.

# Chapter Nine

Turns out, the real question isn't where to start. It's how to shut my mouth. Because as soon as I start talking to this hunky therapist whose eyes are focused on me, I feel an intense need to tell him everything.

Maybe it's the rum punch. Maybe it's because I've kept so

much inside for so long. Or maybe it's because this therapist seems so interested in everything I'm saying.

Halfway through I blurt out, "The worst part is Marcus and I hardly had sex."

There! I finally told someone.

"God, is it because I'm not physically attractive? Like am I ugly?" I cringe at how pitiful I sound.

I start crying. Like ugly crying. With huge gulps of air and big blows of my nose on the crumpled napkin I'd saved. The one holding the tiny umbrellas and plastic swords. They tumble out onto the sand as I blow my nose.

The therapist picks them up and looks at them curiously.

I wave a hand in the air. "They're from my drinks. I . . . think they're pretty. Festive. This was supposed to be . . . a celebration. Not me alone trying to convince everyone and myself that I'm happy I'm single again. Because I'm *not*!" I wail.

He kneels on the sand and rubs circles on my back. The warmth of his hand on my bare skin stops my tears.

Are therapists supposed to touch you like this?

I peek up at him from between the fingers covering my eyes.

A frown puckers his beautiful forehead.

"What do you think?" I ask. "Am I pathetic? That's why Marcus doesn't want me?"

He shakes his head. A wayward curl flips onto his forehead. I so want to smooth it away. Maybe play with it first.

*CJ! Focus.*

"He sounds like a jackass." The sing-song voice roils with disbelief. And a tad bit of anger. "What a first-class jerk."

Are therapists supposed to get angry on your behalf?

Never mind. I lean backward to feel the full effect of his large hand through the thin fabric of my dress. I'm pathetic. But I don't care.

"I haven't told anyone that. I was too embarrassed. It's humiliating, don't you think?"

"I don't have any experience with that," he says.

"Right, none of your clients had issues with their partner not being sexually attracted to them. I'm the only one?"

I wish I could disappear. Here's a therapist who counsels couples and he's never heard of this before.

At that moment, his phone rings.

"Excuse me," he says, standing back up.

I nod miserably. I will gladly pay this man for more of his time. He's a very good listener.

"Okay, I'll be right down," he says.

He slips the phone inside his jacket pocket and reaches down both hands to me. "Come, let me help you up."

I take his hands and allow myself to be pulled up.

Once standing, I see he's even taller than I thought. At least six foot two. A virtual giant to me.

He smiles down at me. "What's your name?"

I grimace. "Sorry. I didn't tell you that first. Or what I do. I'm an intelligent woman. I swear."

"The important thing is whether you feel any better."

I assess myself from head to toe. Inside and out.

"I do. Thank you. Those rum punches made it easy to share."

"Exactly what I like to hear." His teeth glow in the dark. "Can you find your way back to the resort? Just follow the lighted path. Don't stray off the path."

"Famous last words," I joke. "Enjoy the wedding. Will I see you again? Where is your office?"

He points in the direction I came. "I think we will be seeing *a lot* of each other."

I blink. What does he mean? Am I so emotionally unhealthy that I need a lot of therapy while I'm here?

But I don't ask. He's off. Smiling and waving as he skips down the sandy hill toward the wedding. Part of me wishes he'd invited me to go with him.

I trip along the lighted path back to the bar and the resort. The path is much easier than the loose sand I trudged through earlier. I must have been very intoxicated to have missed this path.

From now on I'm staying away from the rum punches. I'll sip only sparkling water with lime.

I pass the beach bar on my way to my golf cart. I wave to Dex who asks if I ran into Keston Kips.

"No, I didn't see the bartender," I smile. "But I did meet your amazing in-house therapist. He needs a raise."

The last thing I see as I climb into my golf cart is Dex's puzzled face. He's saying something like, "*What* therapist?"

I don't respond. I'm not about to discuss my personal problems with an employee working at the bar!

"Good night, Dex." I press on the gas pedal and pull away as a huge yawn overtakes my face.

I keycode myself into my villa. The lights are on. The a/c is blaring cool air. Chocolates are perched on the pillows.

Nice!

It's easy to get used to the luxury of this palatial resort villa. And now I can enjoy it.

The therapist has gotten me to open up in a way that feels like I'm clearing out the old and making room for the new.

And that feeling makes my heart a little lighter and freer.

I'd say the first day of this epic vacation is a win-win.

<h1 style="text-align:center">Chapter Ten</h1>

I wake up to the vacation scent of coconut oil and salty sea air. Even with the a/c purring, I can hear the constant sound of waves smacking the shore. It's the most relaxing sound ever.

Either that or I feel better after talking over my problems with the mysterious therapist last night. I'll have to go find him.

To thank him. Not because he's the most gorgeous guy here. But because his calm listening skills and his outrage on my behalf were remarkably what I needed.

"I can't explain it," I tell Giselle on a video call. "It was as if he could feel my anguish."

Giselle can only nod as she runs on the treadmill. Normally, I'd be running on a treadmill too at the same time instead of preparing to lie out at the pool with a book.

"I think I'll sign up for some formal sessions," I continue. "Unless he wants to meet on the dune again, which is fine with me."

Giselle laughs and gives me a thumbs-up. "Go get your therapist, girl."

I frown. "It's not like that. I'm not interested in him as a *man*."

The smirk on my best friend's face tells me she doesn't believe me for a second.

"It's true," I protest.

She presses the pause button on her machine. "Whatever you say, CJ. I'm happy you're talking to someone. And even happier it's a new man. Did you get his credentials? Where is he licensed?"

I shake my head. "No, but I presume since the resort hired him, he's legit."

"Send me a pic of you guys in your 'counseling' session.'" Giselle does air quotes and I shake my head annoyed.

"I'm not taking his photo while he's working. That would be . . . um . . . ," I actually wouldn't mind getting a pic of him. From what I recall, even in my semi-intoxicated state, he was swoon-worthy.

Geez, I sound like a teenager in my head. Thank God no one can read my mind.

"Fine," I say pretend grudgingly. "I'll see what I can do."

Giselle and I throw kisses at each other and hang up.

As I shower and dress, I hum along to a reggae song I heard a few times last night.

I spin around in the mirror to check out my beach/pool outfit. A slinky pink-hued dress over a pale pink one-piece with cut-out sides. Another birthday present courtesy of my best friends.

I examine the back and sigh. Stuff is hanging out that wasn't there twenty years ago. Despite yoga, spin classes three times per week, and running on the treadmill, I can't stop gravity.

Oh well, it is what it is.

I bend down and scan under the bed for my fluffy mules. They can take any outfit from fun to fabulous.

I suddenly recall I left them at the beach bar when I went walking on the sand. I'll have to track them down at the front desk or maybe they're still at the bar.

I smooth down my wavy hair and apply mascara and lip gloss, just a tiny bit because I'll be hanging out by the pool and beach most of the day and I don't want to look overly made up. The heat down here is no joke.

Plus, I said I didn't want to participate in any activities, but who knows? Maybe a game of volleyball or something would be fun. I used to be a great player back in my day.

*Right CJ.* Like twenty years ago! Ha!

I wonder how old the therapist is. He looked to be in his thirties. Maybe mid-thirties. Whatever . . . age is not important here. I need him to *treat* me professionally. Not to *date* me personally.

I bite my lower lip thinking of the incredible body lurking under that tuxedo. Don't be desperate CJ. Even if you haven't had any in a while. That's no reason to be lusting after the first island man you've met.

Dex doesn't count as he's a baby. Barely twenty-one.

I grab my beach bag, slip on a pair of gold flip-flops, and stroll outside to a day of sunshine and blue skies.

I snap a photo and send it to my friends. "Welcome to Paradise," I comment.

I instantly get back hearts and smiley faces. I can't help the silly smile that creeps across my face. You'd think we were still in college the way we communicate.

I see text messages from Mom on my phone, but I decide to skip them for now. She forgets I'm forty years old. Old enough to spend a few days without her checking up on me.

Trying to placate Mom is almost a full-time job. She wasn't happy I was leaving the country. "Especially while you're vulnerable, Carmela," she'd said. I didn't argue with her. Just told her I was doing what's best for me and I hope she understands.

Of course, she didn't.

I'm only now feeling a bit of positivity in my life. I don't want to read messages that could bring me down again.

<h1 style="text-align:center">Chapter Eleven</h1>

Without even trying, I run into the sexy therapist sooner than expected.

He's at the beach bar. He's wearing a polo shirt with the name of the resort printed on it, khaki shorts that do all kinds of amazing things to his butt and thighs, and canvas shoes.

And can we talk about his calves?

My weakness.

*CJ, you're shameless.* You just broke up with your man and you're drooling over another.

I switch my gaze to the wooden bar counter. So, I don't look creepy.

It's made from slabs of driftwood. It's wonky-looking in a carefree artistic way. Like it's saying, "Who cares what the counter looks like? You're on vacation on a tropical island. We use what we have."

Carved coconut shells hang from the ceiling of the bar overflowing with the brightest green limes I've ever seen. Some are as large as my fist.

The female bartender from last night is behind the bar, blending a pink concoction.

She peels a banana and tosses it in. Blends it some more then pours a bit into a cup and hands it to the therapist. He takes a sip and nods approvingly. Gives the woman a thumbs up. He turns to walk away and sees me standing there.

A big smile fills his face. As if he's truly happy to see me.

My heart pings with excitement.

*Dial down, CJ. He's working here.*

I do a silly close-to-the-body wave. Like my hand is glued to my chest.

I feel my face smiling back at him, invitingly.

He steps toward me. "Hi there. How are you feeling?" Oh, that sing-song accent is so sexy and sweet.

I debate whether to jump straight to booking sessions with him or just chit-chat about how I feel, which is undetermined right now.

I decide not to rush things. I'm here for two weeks, I'm sure I can book sessions at the front desk.

"I'm doing better, thank you," I smile and feel my face

getting hot. I can't remember everything I told him last night. But I know it was a lot.

"That's wonderful. I told you I might be able to help."

I nod vigorously. "You did help."

Dex appears, holding my shoes in one hand. "Miss, you forgot these. I kept them behind the bar for you."

I close my eyes. *Damn Dex, way to go making me look irresponsible.*

The therapist reaches for them. Holds them up in his strong-looking hand. "Very pretty."

"Thanks," I mumble turning as red as my brown complexion allows.

I reach for them, but he carries them to the golf cart I'd parked at the edge of the sand. He puts them in the basket on the back.

I follow him admiring his powerful calf muscles. Unlike me, he's been walking in the sand every day for a long time. He turns and catches me staring. A smile lights up his entire face.

He's got to be the happiest counselor I've ever seen.

Without stopping to think I hold up my phone and switch to selfie mode. "Want to take a picture with me?" I ask.

For a couple of seconds, he doesn't say anything. I desperately want to turn and run. I've overstepped the counselor/client boundary. Such a rookie move.

And I'm a damn lawyer. I should know better.

But then, like a curtain being raised to reveal the wizard, his face changes.

A smirk lifts his lips upward at one corner of his mouth. He leans down, puts an arm around my shoulders, and says, "Sure. For your social media, right?"

No, it's for me. But I don't say that. I snap two photos and tuck my phone into my bag. "Thanks."

We stare at each other.

*Awkward!*

I drop my eyes to the embroidered *Cocoa Reef Resort* on his chest.

"Um . . . ," I start.

He stays still.

"My name is Carmela." I clear my throat. "Carmela Jones, but everyone calls me CJ."

Everyone except my mother and my ex-boyfriend, I think. He doesn't need to know all that. At least not right now. "Can I book some sessions with you?" I clear my throat again. So much for waiting until later. Standing so close to this man is unnerving me.

"Sessions? Do you like sessions? Not many visitors know about them."

I frown. What the hell is he talking about?

At that moment, the woman behind the bar turns up the music. A Beenie Man song blares highly suggestive lyrics that make me blush. Because ahem . . . *"pon bed pon floor against wall."* Then the next song, *"mek me bawl and cry."*

He's smiling at me. "You sure you want to go to a session with me? You can barely stand here and tek it."

That's when it hits me. A session is island slang for a "party." He thinks I want to go to a party with him. Either that or he's joking around. That must be it.

"I'm sure," I laugh, throwing one arm wide. "Why not?"

"Irie," he says. "We'll catch a session this week."

Vacationing couples start filling up the tables and chairs.

"I'm sorry, CJ," he says. "I have to get to work."

"Of course," I say, stepping out of his way.

He pats my arm. "I'd love to see you later. How about nine o'clock?"

"Nine? At night?"

"Yes, I'll be off work then and I can focus all my attention on you." He grants me that sexy, carefree smile again.

"Sure, where should we meet?"

He points to the bar. "I'll be right here most of the day. You can hang out now or come find me here later."

I nod slowly as questions swirl through my head.

Does he do his counseling at the bar?

Is that an *activity* on the schedule?

The schedule I crumpled and threw in the waste basket in my room yesterday.

I could always amble over to the reception area and ask for another one.

Nah! I'll grab a snack and sparkling water and plop down on a beach chair under one of these shady coconut trees.

"What's your name?" I manage to shout as he walks toward the bar. "I'm sorry I didn't catch it last night."

He turns in mid-stride. Sexy calf muscles pop out like bricks.

I gulp. Steady CJ. He's your therapist, remember. You've already crossed some lines and now you're ogling him in public.

He grins as if he's reading my mind

"You're cute, you know that, CJ. Very *very* cute."

"Thank you." I blush for real now. Counselor/client boundaries be damned.

At that moment, Dex walks by bearing a tray of colorful drinks with cute umbrellas looking all perky.

"I want one of those," I say, forgetting my promise not to drink alcohol today.

Dex waves his free hand at the bar. "Why don't you ask the expert? You'll get the absolute best drink."

"Which expert?" I ask confused.

"Keston Kips, of course. I see you've finally met him."

I stare. "I have?"

Dex keeps walking. "I gotta get these folks their drinks. Grab a seat."

But I don't sit down. Because my eyes are peeled to the bar.

The therapist has gone behind the driftwood counter. He's setting up blenders, three of them all in a row. He's taking limes out of the hanging baskets.

Is he *juggling the limes*? WTF?

"Hey Keston," Dex calls out as he sails by me with an empty tray. "Can you make this fine young lady your Pirate's Cove Punch, please?"

"You got it," the therapist calls back. Except . . . he's *not* a therapist!

He's shaking a metal canister and pouring drinks into glasses.

I can't move. I never knew what people meant when they said they were *floored*.

But I'm frozen in place. I literally can't pick my feet up off the floor. This must be what it means.

At that moment, the therapist, also known as Keston Kips, looks over at me and shuts one eyelid down. As it pops up, I realize the man is *winking* at me.

The effing nerve. The fraudster. The lunatic. Then it hits me fully.

I told *the bartender* all my personal business. About how I'm lonely. And feeling used and abandoned. I told him I was sex-starved!

The BARTENDER!?

"Oh fuck," I groan. "Oh fuck, fuck, fuck." I've now, without a doubt, hit rock bottom.

# Chapter Twelve

**M**y blood is boiling, and not from the hot Caribbean sunshine. I feel as if my blood vessels may actually pop with the indignation and anger surging through me.

Once I recover my ability to walk, I race away from the bar

and the humiliation. I fast step it down the beach toward the furthest beach chair, and away from that awful Keston Kips.

But I can't sit. I yank my phone out of the beach bag. My feet stomp the sand back and forth digging two trenches as I press Giselle's number.

Please let her be available, I silently pray.

"Yo, you showing off with your blue sea and white sand while I freeze my buns off up here?"

"No. Giselle, something horrible happened."

Her face changes in an instant., "What? Do you need a doctor? An EMT? A police officer?"

At the sound of her love-filled voice, I burst into tears. My emotions are all over the place.

"No, it's about the therapist. Fake therapist, I mean."

"I'm calling the others."

They appear one by one. Katana is at home. Lisa is in her office surrounded by maps of the galaxies. Giselle is now in her car in the parking lot, which is where she takes our calls. And Mikah is . . . um.

"Girl, are you in a hotel room?" asks Lisa. "Cause that ain't your bed."

Mikah stretches like a cat rising out from the covers. She's a freelance model. She works when she gets called and she gets called a lot. In her spare time, she loves her sugar daddies.

"I thought we're here for CJ. My location is irrelevant."

"She's right. This is about CJ. Something's happened." Giselle takes charge.

They all stare from their devices and wait for me to speak.

"I'm such a fool."

"Now now," says Katana in her full motherly role. "What-ever it is, we can sort it out."

I blubber. "It's the bartender. He pretended to be a thera-pist last night and I confessed all my painful secrets. Stuff about me and Marcus and how I felt rejected and . . ." I sniff. "I don't know what to do. I'm so embarrassed."

Dead silence.

Giselle is the first to speak. "I'm not going to say I told you so. Because you were too excited this morning."

"Wait, fill us in," shouts Katana. "I want all the deets."

I spend the next ten minutes relaying my meeting on the sand dune with the tuxedo-clad man. How he said he was a therapist. And the awful dumping of all my personal baggage on the sand. For him to sift through.

"Ah ha!" Mikah says. "You worry too much CJ. You were drinking. You got stuff off your chest. Now you can ignore him. He served a good purpose as far as I'm concerned."

"What purpose is that?" I bawl.

Mikah shrugs her fine-boned shoulders. Tosses her slinky long black hair. "You needed a stranger to listen to you. Think of it as confessing your deepest darkest secrets on a transatlantic flight. Now it's done. Forget him. Move on."

"She can't do that. He works at the resort." Katana rudely sucks her teeth at Mikah.

"Exactly," I say. "It's humiliating. I'm thinking I should report him. To the resort manager."

Four faces stare back at me aghast.

"Report him?" Lisa says in a highly skeptical tone. "Girlfriend, think rationally. You can't go reporting a working man for listening to your problems. You're gonna make him lose his job. Is that what you want?"

"Yes," I say defiantly.

Giselle snorts. "You're not reporting anybody, do you hear me."

Did I mention Giselle is a principal of a prestigious middle school in Brooklyn? It got prestigious under her watch; it didn't start that way.

"But you guys didn't see the wink he gave me. And he called me 'very cute.' He's probably laughing his head off at me right now."

Katana gawks. "A man calls you very cute and winks at you and you're mad? God, I miss the days of a man doing those things with me."

"You have a fantastic hubby, stop complaining," Mikah says.

Katana rubs her swollen abdomen. "It's not the same thing. I'm a vessel right now. I miss being small and cute and perky."

We all say sweet things to Katana to remind her that after she delivers, she'll have the best present of all. A small, cute, perky newborn.

Katana rolls her eyes at us. "Let's focus on CJ's terrible problem."

I realize they're not taking this seriously. "It's not funny, you know."

"Is he at least hot?" asks Mikah. "He'd better be. Or this is a waste of our time."

I send them the selfie I took this morning.

"I took it before I knew he'd lied and tricked me."

Katana pretends to wipe sweat from her brow. "Whoa!"

Mikah grins. "I knew it. You wouldn't care if he were dog food."

I throw her a nasty glare. "Don't be shallow. And yes, I'd feel the same regardless of his looks."

Giselle is staring hard at the screen where the photo is posted. She points a red-tipped nail. "I've seen his face before, CJ."

I frown. "Where?"

"In my dreams!"

Everyone but me laughs.

I bite my lip. "His looks are not important. He betrayed my confidence by pretending to be a professional counselor."

My girls all nod their heads.

"There's only one thing you can do," Giselle says.

"What?" we ask.

"You must give him a time-out. No communication. No hanging out where he is. And no more alone time with him. He's obviously using his good looks to create a trust bond."

"But for what purpose?"

Mikah snaps her fingers. "He's looking for a sugar mama."

I groan.

Lisa covers her mouth with one hand. "You could be right."

"You should know, Mikah." Katana laughs.

Mikah glares at her. "I'm just saying . . . it's an exclusive resort with very wealthy guests. He probably thinks CJ is wealthy too."

"Which I'm not. And he doesn't think I'm rich because I confessed that I stole Marcus's tickets to get here."

"Hmmm . . . maybe he wants to have sex. You're a beautiful woman." Lisa eyes her ceiling, which is how she contemplates interplanetary problems. I should be honored Lisa is giving me a bit of her precious brain matter.

"Are you saying he's trying to help me get my groove back?"

Everyone but me burst out laughing. Again.

"We didn't know it was missing," Katana chuckles.

"Bingo!" Mikah says, pointing her finger at me in a gun salute. "I'd ignore Giselle's advice and get busy with this hunk. You've got two weeks to reset your inner goddess power then fly out."

"So, I should *use* him?"

Mikah shrugs. "It's not using if you're two consenting adults. Then it's called, 'having fun.'"

"Don't forget the condoms," yells Katana. "Whatever you do."

I shake my head. "You all are ridiculous. I called for sympathy. Instead, you're telling me to bang the man who conned me."

Mikah sighs. "See this as a positive development. This guy got you to switch from grieving about Marcus to feeling something else."

"Feeling mad!" I snort. But I get what Mikah is saying. Keston Kips managed to do something no one could do for weeks. He got me to stop thinking about Marcus and focus on something else.

I'm not sure what exactly I feel now.

But it's not sadness.

# Chapter Thirteen

"Oh shoot. Girls, he's walking down the beach. He's heading toward my chair. I gotta go."

"Turn your phone around," Katana yells. "I want to live through you."

"She'll do no such thing," Giselle corrects. "Let CJ handle her business."

"But call us as soon as he leaves," Lisa says.

"I'll tell you everything later," I promise.

"Remember your inner goddess needs some loving," Mikah shouts as I slide my phone into the bag.

My ears are burning up and it's not from the sun. Keston Kips is standing right in front of me. I'm sure he heard Mikah's parting words. He looks as if he's trying to hide a smirk and failing.

"I made this especially for you." He has the nerve to try to hand me a drink. I hate to say this but it's the most enchanting cocktail I've ever seen.

Still, I do not take it. I clasp my arms across my chest. My weight shifts to my back leg and I strike a "Yeah, what do you want?" pose.

For good measure, I tap my outstretched foot impatiently. It's not effective because it makes no sound as it sinks into the powdery sand.

I lift it up pretending that was my intention all along.

"I don't want any drink from you."

"Please take it."

It's the way he says, 'please' that stops me.

"Why should I? You lied to me."

He doesn't deny it. Just pushes the drink closer to me.

"It was made with love."

I squish up one side of my mouth.

"Yeah, right."

I look inside the tall fancy glass. A moon slice of the yellowest pineapple swirls on a sea-green foam. A fragrant coconut scent drifts to my nostrils. Flower petals and something I don't recognize decorate the sides of the glass.

"That's a star fruit," he says, pointing at the strange object as if reading my thoughts.

"What's in this drink? You trying to poison me?"

He laughs out loud. "For that, I'd use oleanders. But no, this is innocent."

"Unlike the bartender who made it."

He grins in that boyish way he did last night. The smile that caught me in this web of deceit. His secret weapon.

"Take a sip," he says.

I sniff the glass. "What's in it?"

"Two ounces of apology, one cup of zipped lips (he imitates zipping his lips shut), and a dash of hope."

I roll my eyes, refusing to smile. He doesn't deserve it.

"What's the hope for?"

"That we'll be friends. Please come back to the beach bar. You don't have to sit all the way over here. We're starting a volleyball game soon."

"I'll think about it."

I bend my head and take a tiny sip of the drink, which is cold and frothy and . . . wow!

I bite my bottom lip. This man is a *genius* at mixing cocktails. But I'm not going to feed his ego. I tilt my head and look up from under my eyelashes.

"It's a'ight."

He stares at me. "Cool."

He knows I'm lying. I can't wait for him to go so I can suck this liquid gold down to the last dregs.

As he turns to leave, I ask, "Why'd you do it? Why'd you pretend to be a therapist? Is that your party trick? Your way of getting women to open up to you? So you'll have the upper hand?"

He frowns. It's the first time I've seen anything but twinkly eyes and sunshine on his face. "Do I have the upper hand with you?" he asks. "Because it doesn't feel like it."

My shoulders drop.

"No," I agree. "But still . . . it was a terrible thing to do. I thought I was talking to a real therapist."

His brown eyes soften. "I'm sorry. I tried to tell you. You kept talking so I listened. I thought that's what you needed. Someone to listen."

"Yeah . . . well . . . you should have spoken up louder and made sure I knew."

"I didn't imagine you believed I was a real therapist. It's a resort, not rehab."

I snort.

"It was probably the tuxedo."

"What was the tuxedo?"

"If I was dressed in my usual after-work clothes—shorts and a t-shirt—you'd have ignored me. You'd never think I was a therapist."

"That's not true."

His turn to squish up his mouth at me.

We both know he's right.

"So now you're calling me a snob?"

"I don't know you well enough to call you that. I'm just stating facts about one situation."

"Whoa, you'd make a great lawyer."

"I think we've established I'm just a bartender."

Something in the way he says that makes me stop in my tracks. Why am I fighting with this guy? He's working. At a resort. Where I'm on a vacation that costs *thousands* of dollars.

"I have to get back to the beach bar. But I hope you'll come join us for some volleyball." He takes two strides, then stops and turns back around to face me. My eyes are on the melting ice in my drink. I was so engrossed in my heated debate with the bartender that my drink lost its fizzle and pop.

"Even if you don't want to play volleyball," he says, "come back and I'll make you another one of those drinks."

His smile outshines the damn sun. It's as if he owns the light on this Caribbean Island.

"Maybe."

I have no intention of going anywhere near Keston Kips again. From now on, if I want one of his phenomenal drinks, I'll order it from Dex. Better yet, from room service.

# Chapter Fourteen

I spend the rest of the morning traipsing in and out of the blue ocean. The waves try to drag me out, but I maintain my toe grips on the dazzling pink sand.

It doesn't escape me that I'm alone in my corner of the beach. There's no lifeguard on duty, which is posted on signs, and no other guests hanging about.

I'm in my own world. The coconut palms sway in the breeze. Their fronds make artistic shadow designs on the sand. Screeching green birds, which I later find out are parrots, *duh*, fly by in pairs overhead.

The sound of water behind me captures my attention. I follow the sound to find a river flowing over bleached white rocks toward the sea.

I wish Marcus could see it.

What the hell am I thinking? Has the sun gotten to me?

I've discovered a real-life paradise. The last thing I need to be thinking about is my ex-boyfriend.

I perch on a large white boulder, knees drawn up under my chin, and contemplate the river. It has its own ecosystem going on. Tiny brown frogs, black fish, and snails all live here. I'm the intruder with my splashing feet and island radio station cranking Bob Marley on my iPhone.

"It's me and you, Bob," I speak aloud.

I'm taking pleasure in immersing myself in my private world and ignoring the gourmet snacks, drinks, and activities. Part of it, I must admit, is showing Keston Kips I don't need him or his fancy drinks.

But as Tom Hanks's character in *Cast Away* can tell you, everyone needs human companionship.

So, after leaving the river, I drag my beach chair under a canopy of coconut tree branches and slide my sunblock-protected body into the perfect reading position. Tom Hanks' character had a volleyball. I have a book.

My stomach growls as lunchtime comes and goes while I turn the pages of one of the books on my TBR lists. I've brought ten books, anticipating lots of free time to relax and dive into other worlds and other people's problems.

And I do try.

I really do. But my mind keeps drifting back to the restaurant and Marcus's face, clear as the river water, when he said marriage to me was not on his agenda. Not now. Not anytime soon. Well, he didn't say that last part, but his eyes, which stared at me with pity, might as well have.

The book falls in my lap. I drop my face into my hands.

*How could I be so dumb?*

Maybe it's the sun. The sea. The lack of sleep for two weeks. But thick salty tears slide down my face and onto my lips. I press my fingers tightly to hold the tears back.

What does it matter?

There's no one around to hear me cry.

No one around for me to be brave for.

All the trash-talking I did with my girlfriends means nothing.

The truth is, Marcus didn't want me.

And the question that streams on repeat in my head is, "Why not?"

# Chapter Fifteen

I dream of the river. The rushing song of water hitting rocks and flowing in mini torrents toward the big wide sea. I'm swimming with the current, escaping the darkness of a forest. Sunshine and blue skies beckon.

A giant roar fills my ears.

What the hell? I sit bolt upright in bed. Shove the sleep

mask up on my forehead. I look around wildly. The roar is closer now. Coming from inside my room.

My eyes find the bedside phone.

The roar comes again.

I stare at the phone. By the time it roars again, I'm holding the receiver. It's been a long time since I used a regular phone.

"Hello?" I ask. "Can I help you?"

"Mrs. O'Brien," comes the sweet sound of an islander. "We have you scheduled for the coastline cruise leaving our dock at ten a.m. This is a reminder to be on the dock fifteen minutes before, please."

She lost me at 'Mrs. O'Brien.'

I square my shoulders. Squeeze my eyes shut. "I am not Mrs. O'Brien," I say softly. My heart slams like the lid on a hope chest.

"Oh, I'm sorry." I hear her fingers clacking on a keyboard. She must be checking to see who I am and whether I belong here.

"My name is Carmela Jones. Mr. O'Brien made the reservation. I am the other guest on this reservation."

"Yes, I see that. Sorry, Ms. Jones. But will you be going on the boat cruise?" Her voice rises like red robins taking flight from a clothesline.

"No thank you. I won't be taking the boat tour."

Before she can say anything else, I add extra politely, "But thank you."

It's not *her* fault I'm not Mrs. O'Brien.

"No worries. I'll cross you off the list. If you change your mind, please stop by the front desk."

"Okay, I'll do that."

After hanging up, I survey the sunken living area, with its overstuffed cushions and cheery pillows. The patio with its empty hammock, luxurious lounge chairs, and view of the sea in the distance.

"I can't go on a romantic boat cruise by myself," I mutter. It's probably one of those swanky cruises with silver-haired couples cuddled up, the breeze blowing in their hair, not a care in the world. The total opposite of me.

My brown arms and legs are deepening in color. Upon arriving at St. Nicholas, I looked like a latte. Now, my skin is a robust espresso, on its way to black coffee. I laugh at my reflection in the mirror wishing I could share this joke with my girls.

We all belong to a Diverse Voices romance book club. Brown skin is constantly being compared to cinnamon, coffee, caramel, and cocoa as if we're flavors. But I can't bother them while they're working two days in a row.

After showering, I shimmy into another designer swimsuit. This one is an iridescent peacock blue-green and shows off my tanned skin.

I pull out the exquisite matching beach cover-up created from crocheted silk. Filaments of gold thread weave in and out of the delicate yarn. I slip it over the two-piece suit. It hugs my bosom, cinches at my waist, and flows down to my toes.

I spin around in the mirror. This dress could be worn to a Cinderella ball. It's that beautiful.

The face in the mirror frowns.

Who am I kidding? The clothes don't make me feel as if I'm celebrating my singledom. They remind me of Marcus's epic rejection. Out of nowhere, hot tears threaten to fall.

"Enough," I reprimand myself walking briskly towards the door. "You're going to have a perfect day."

I gather my beach bag, throw in sunblock, bug spray, and a Kennedy Ryan romance from my TBR pile. Pink designer sunglasses perch like a crown on my head.

I swish out the room with a hip swivel to rival any Rihanna music video.

# Chapter Sixteen

"Girl, how are you looking good enough to eat?"

It's the teasing voice of Keston Kips. Why must he be the first person I run into as I park my golf cart?

I swing my beach bag over one shoulder, roll my eyes, and keep walking. He'll get the message.

"I made you something very special," he says, smiling brightly. He's walking backward in front of me so he can see my face. "Let me go get it from the fridge."

"Are you always this happy?"

He nods. "Of course. Aren't you?"

I suck my teeth. "I thought it was only babies and fools who found life amusing all the time."

He stops walking abruptly. I can't stop my momentum and I end up with my face smack against his chest.

"Damn, sorry," he says as he grabs me in his arms. "Are you hurt?"

His chest is solid. Like a rock face with ridges. This probably means that on top of everything else, he's super cut under his shirt. How annoying is that?

"No," I try and step back, but he's got his hands on my waist to steady me. They slide down my sides in a warm gentle sweep, large fingers pressing through the crocheted fabric.

He hooks two fingers into either side of the dress and pulls me close. "I won't let you fall." Deep brown eyes bore into mine. I can't look away. I find myself tumbling into the depths of his gaze.

With great effort, I snap myself out of the hypnosis that is Keston Kips.

"I don't need your help." I push against his chest. God, he feels so good. So muscled and hard.

As my top half leans backward, my bottom half presses closer to his body. That's when I feel it.

The motherlode of all motherlodes. My crotch grazes it. Presses on it.

WTF!

Hot dampness fills my pussy. I stiffen in his arms.

Can he tell?

Oh lawd. My brand-new bikini bottoms are getting

drenched. If he keeps holding me like this, I'll be coming right here in the garden.

I push him away. My breath comes in short halting bursts. This man is fire. Burning my skin.

"What's wrong?" he asks.

"Nothing."

But I can't look him in the eye. His pure masculinity has rammed through my dormant femininity.

Just standing next to him makes me want to drag him back to my room and do all kinds of salacious things to him on the thick bedroom carpet. On the luxury cushions. In the giant marble bathtub.

I gulp.

He tilts his head. "Don't move. Let me get that breakfast smoothie I whipped up for you. Are you drinking enough water? You look thirsty."

If he only knew the thirst I'm feeling is for his body. His fine, tall, hard body.

What's wrong with me? I don't even *like* him.

I recall something Mikah told us once. "You don't have to like a man to have a deep soulful satisfying sexual connection."

We all thought she was just sex crazy.

Then she'd said, "If you're vibrating on the same frequency, then wham!" She'd slapped her hands hard together. "Your body will cream for his candy stick."

The way Mikah spoke, none of us took her seriously. But this may have some truth to it.

Because when Keston Kips touches me, my entire body whimpers. Begs for more.

As he strides toward the bar, I can't take my eyes off his back muscles rippling through his fitted polo shirt. Or his firm butt in the khaki shorts. Or those veiny muscled calves.

I fan myself with one hand.

I've got to get out of here. I'm clearly suffering from delusions. Or sunstroke. Maybe even *Stella-itis*.

I look left. I look right.

Usually, there are colorful signposts directing guests to various parts of the resort grounds.

Where's the one directing guests to the dock?

I need to get on that coastline cruise right now. To get as far away as possible from the resort. From the beach bar. From Keston Kips.

And his frequency.

Before I get my groove on with the young bartender.

# Chapter Seventeen

I give a huge sigh of relief when I locate the dock and see a large catamaran with *Cocoa Reef Resort* painted on its side tied to the dock.

Passengers are being helped into the boat by two strong young men wearing shirts wth "Crew" written on the backs. Is hot body a hiring requirement here?

An older man with a pirate hat—it looks real to me—is greeting guests and posing for photos.

I scramble to join the line of guests.

When I get to the front, I give my name and Villa number.

There's a bit of confusion as they tell me that my name is not on their list. I remember that I canceled my reservation. I explain that I changed my mind.

"I'd really like to go now though, if that's okay."

The young man who looks to be in his early twenties waves me on board. "You're not on the list, but we don't turn away pretty women."

I blush. "Thanks. I swear I paid for the boat trip already. I canceled my reservation this morning by mistake."

He nods. "No problem."

I find a seat on the white ledge in front of the netted section where most of the guests have congregated.

I was wrong. It's not mostly older couples.

There's a nice mix of ages. There are older couples, yes, but also many young people swaying to the music blaring over the boat speakers.

Rum punches are being handed around. Before I know it, the boat lines are untied, the crew jumps aboard from the dock and the pirate captain gives us instructions.

"I only have three rules. One, don't throw anything in the water. Two, when we dock don't wander off and miss the return boat." People cheer to that.

"And three, have a great time. I'm driving the boat so sit back, drink up, and enjoy yourself."

More loud cheers. I join in that last one. Why else am I here if not to follow those instructions to a T.

"Are you visiting our island by yourself?" asks the crew member who let me come aboard even though my name wasn't on his list.

I shrug. "It didn't start off that way, but yes, now I am."

He winks. "Why bring sand to the beach, right?"

I laugh nervously. "Exactly."

He hands me a rum punch. I take a sip and recognize it immediately as a Keston Kips special. He must have made up a batch for the trip. Perfect. I can enjoy his drinks and not have to see him.

As the boat plunges through the waves leaving the shoreline behind, I exhale. Seriously, this isn't so hard. I thought I'd be super embarrassed being by myself. But no one seems to think it's weird that I'm traveling alone.

I turn my face to the sun after dabbing on a handful of sunblock. The warm sunshine oozes through every bone, muscle, and fiber of my body.

The soothing sound of Bob Marley fills my ears and heart as the crew cranks up the playlist.

With every rise and fall of the waves, my body relaxes more and more. Oh my, I could stay here forever. I don't think I've ever felt so relaxed. I close my eyes and lean back letting the music and the waves hitting the hull cradle me into a peaceful meditation.

"This is the life," I say to no one as my eyelids get heavy.

I must have dozed off. When I open my eyes, I feel a towel tucked behind my head. Probably that sweet young man. I stretch my arms above my head, closing my eyes again.

The soothing sound of reggae is abruptly replaced by a hard, fast danceable music the islanders call soca.

"It's basically sex while dancing," I mutter.

"Well, then, you must come and dance with me."

My eyes snap open.

I sit up.

"What. Are. You. Doing. Here?"

"Making sure you don't burn to death in the sun." Keston Kips' smiling face fills my vision. My gaze drifts downward.

To smooth darkly bronzed skin. I was right. His body is blindingly perfect. It's sickening. Nobody should have this smile and this body and this much confidence. Makes me wonder what he's hiding.

"I thought you had to work."

His face lights up as if he's five and I offered him a bowl of candy. "I *am* working. I'm bartending this cruise. The real question is, what are *you* doing here? I didn't see your name on the passenger manifest."

"It's a mix-up." I wave away the inquiry.

His smile broadens if that's possible. I swear he gives the sun a run for its money. "Look, Keston," I say.

"You know my name," he beams.

I do my best not to roll my eyes. "Thanks for the invite to dance, but I'll just sit here and watch the gorgeous scenery go by."

He shakes his head. "One dance. If you don't like it, you can easily sit back down."

I think about that logic. I glance over at the passengers grooving to the island music.

"It looks like Cancun on Spring Break."

He stands up and reaches for my hand. "It's time you had some fun."

His washboard abs ripple and furrow. I'm as shallow as Mikah the way I'm staring. *Drool much, CJ?*

"How old are you?" I blurt out.

He smirks. "Why?"

I stand on my own power. "Just wondering if I need to card you before we dance."

A laugh erupts from his belly. It makes me smile. A little.

"I was serious."

"Thirty-two."

"I'm forty."

"I love even numbers."

I blink. Does anything affect this guy?

"You're strange."

"Thanks," he says. "I like to think I'm Lucy in the sky with diamonds."

I scratch my head. "Huh?"

"Never mind. Music is waiting. I'll explain another time."

"No. I want to know. Are you talking about the Beatles song? Or some island reference I don't get?"

"Neither. It's a real star in the sky called Lucy. Its carbon core has crystallized to form a diamond of ten billion trillion trillion carats."

"Whoa." He has my attention now.

"Astronomers call her Lucy, after the Beatles' song."

"And you identify with it? Because you're like a . . . *diamond*?"

His lips quirk up one side.

I can't help but stare as he explains about him and Lucy being born (or discovered) in the same year, 1992.

Part of me is fascinated to learn this trivia about astronomy. The other part is wondering, who is this dude? For real.

"So will you dance with me now?" he finishes.

"Sure, *Lucy*."

My feet follow on their own accord. My mind is still dissecting his fascination with stars.

Besides, he's right. It's just a dance. I'm not committing to anything. I put my beach bag on top of the center console along with the other bags.

The music is pumping hard. Suggestive lyrics like "look back at me." I stare at the bold women gyrating, bending over, and wiggling their bottoms in the air.

"I don't dance like that," I say over my shoulder to Keston, who is now behind me, hands on my hips. The line between his touch and the space he's giving me to move is as thin as the gold threads in my crochet dress.

"Dance like yourself."

"I've seen how you islanders dance. You give dirty dancing a new meaning."

Keston laughs his deep laugh. It's infectious. It almost makes me want to laugh too. But I'm not ready to forgive him for pretending to be a therapist while I revealed my pain and rejection.

He knows I haven't been doing the nasty with my own long-term boyfriend! How humiliating is that. This is probably a pity dance. As soon as it's over I'm sitting my ass back down. Let him discuss Lucy with a willing tourist.

At that moment, a gorgeous suntanned guest I've seen around the resort glides over to me, her eyes on the man behind my back. "How did you pull the bartender, girl?"

I respond like Jonathan Owens when he was asked how he pulled the greatest athlete in the world today, Simone Biles.

"You mean how did *the bartender* pull me?"

"Ohhh," her eyes widen. "Nice. Can I steal him away when you're done?"

Keston's arm tightens around my waist. As if he's conveying to me that he's not going anywhere.

"I'll think about it."

She nods and points to where she and some other women are hanging out. Everyone's eyes are on me. "I'll be over there."

If I cared I would be a bit insulted. Like woman! I'm dancing and you're trying to cut in?

But I don't care that Keston Kips is in high demand. And probably for reasons I don't want to know about.

"Your harem awaits," I say as the song ends.

He gently caresses my shoulder, moving my hair out of the way. His breath is warm on my neck as he whispers, "I'm fine where I am."

The song changes to another thrill-seeking jam. "I can get all my aerobics out of the way on this cruise," I snort as we resume dancing to a heart-racing pace.

"*All*?" Keston asks, encircling me with his muscular arms and moving his hips boldly against mine.

I can go with this flow, right? It's not illegal to enjoy a booty grind with this young hot bartender, the most popular man on St. Nick it seems.

"Damn, that feels so good."

"What're you saying?"

I didn't realize I spoke out loud.

"Um . . . I said I need another drink?"

Keston's hips knock my butt hard. It feels like a precursor to a seriously hot sweaty sexual romp. But that's just how they dance here, I remind myself. It's nothing special to him.

"I'll be back. Let me get it for you." He disappears into the crowd.

I turn to watch the green mountains, craggy cliffs, and tiny rocky outposts boasting tall trees in the middle of the sea, looking like perfect pirate hideouts.

St. Nick's is breathtaking just like all the photos and videos showed.

I lean on the rope railing surrounding the boat. This is no ordinary beachy island. The extensive jungle and rainforests are what make St. Nick different from many of the other vacation spots. Old-school conservationists managed to protect half the island from the human population.

"Admiring my home?"

Keston arrives with a cold beverage that I gulp down like it's the last thing I'm ever going to drink.

"Whoa," he says. "That has some serious alcohol in it."

"And?"

He shrugs. "Okay. Next time I'll also bring some water."

I fling my hand outward. "I'm checking out the waterfalls. Can you believe how many waterfalls there are?"

He grins. "Yeah. The island is known for its abundance of waterfalls. I bet we can find one on No Man's Land too."

"Why do you call it that?"

He shrugs. "There's no way to get there except by boat. It's deserted."

I raise my fists and curl my fingers in and out, my hands imitating a scary ghost. "Ooooh. Is it haunted too?"

"Definitely. They say a shipload of pirates were murdered there as they lay sleeping when another pirate ship came upon them. The blood on the beach runs so deep it's known as Bloody Bay."

I blanch. "I was joking."

He grins. "I wasn't."

"Okay, then," I mutter. "This is supposed to be a fun adventure. Not a visit to a massacre."

"Nothing is all rainbows and butterflies, sweetheart. With our island's beauty also comes its tragedies, which include quite a bit of bloodshed, slavery, colonial powers fighting each other for ownership and . . ." He stops. He must have gotten a good look at my eyes, opening wider and wider as I imagine all the pain that has occurred on these beaches and mountains.

He clears his throat. "Never mind. Nobody likes to think about that stuff. Should I get you another drink?"

I nod. "Sure," I whisper. "And I'm sorry I made light of your history."

His broad shoulders raise and drop. "Not to get all philosophical on a booze cruise . . ."

"But you're already there, so . . ."

"We might be a product of our history. But we can write our own future."

He locks eyes with mine.

Is he talking about me, too?

"You're pretty clever, Keston Kips."

A grin lights up his face. "See?"

"See what?"

"That's why they call me a therapist."

I smack my forehead. "Please. Not that again. I'm trying to forget." I push his body away. "You can go now. Let me enjoy the beauty of the island. But thank you for the history lesson. I'm interested in it all."

"I'll be over there if you need me." Keston points to the bar area where the same group of female tourists are looking over here with more than thirst in their eyes.

"Your fandom looks pissed off."

"There's enough of me to go around."

"Ugh! Did you really say that?"

He leans over and whispers. "It's part of the spiel we bartenders must learn to keep all our customers happy. But in your case, I'll try to come up with original lines."

He swaggers off, calf muscles rippling, back muscles glistening, and I swear there's a collective sigh of relief from everyone on board as he approaches the bar.

"What do they know that I don't?" I wonder.

In seconds, the sound of laughter, loud cheering with cups clicking and feet stomping replaces the music.

"To the best bartender in the Caribbean," someone shouts.

"Here, here," others join in.

The man has a talent. I can't deny it.

But he's too young for me. I just got out of a relationship. And I don't do players. Even ones with bursts of wisdom.

All in all, Keston Kips is not a keeper. Not for me. Not even as a vacation fling.

# Chapter Nineteen

No Man's Land belongs in a movie. Or at least a commercial for an exclusive brand. The stretch of white sand, sparkling turquoise water, and emerald green mountains hugging the curve of the beach look unreal. I can't believe this isn't an image conjured up by AI.

At both ends of the half-moon beach are huge rocks you can climb and sit on or dive off into the crystal-clear sea.

All the guests, me included ooh and ahh as we leap off the side of the boat and into the shallow water to wade to the sand. I snap a photo to send to my girls, but there's no WiFi or cell service so I save it for later.

I'm busy gazing around, eyes wide.

The crew quickly sets up a BBQ station and a table laden with ceramic dishes for the island-style picnic.

I peek into the dishes that everyone's digging into. Potato salad, macaroni pie, lentil peas in a delicious smelling sauce. Fried plantains. Rice and peas.

Too much starch for me.

But from the blocks of charcoal comes the aromatic scent of grilled chicken, fresh fish caught by the captain as we sailed here, and lobsters the size of my forearm.

"Oh yeah, I'll have a tiny bit of lobster," I tell the chef.

He smiles and deposits half a crustacean in its shell on my plate. "Caribbean lobster," he says. "Enjoy."

I sit on the edge of the sand and pick at the delicious meal.

Keston Kips wanders by, a line of women following him. He stops at my feet. "That's all you're eating?" he asks when he sees my plate.

I nod.

He makes a *tssk* sound and continues along on his pied piper way. I hear one of the women ask, "Is that your sister?"

"As if," I mutter channeling my inner Cher from *Clueless*.

After my perfect small meal, I wander over to the rocks and sit with my feet in the water.

"We don't even need snorkeling gear to see the fish," a woman remarks pointing downward.

She's right. Darting all about my bare feet are the cutest

black and yellow fish, blue striped fish, and OMG a slinky spotted stingray. Swimming off toward the deep.

I squeal and point at him.

"It's harmless," says a crew member. "But don't try to play with it."

"Noted. No playing with stingrays on the island."

He laughs. "You're Keston's girl, huh?"

My mouth drops open. "I am not."

He shrugs. "If you say so."

Before I can protest more, he one-handedly leaps back onto the boat and gathers up a string bag full of snorkeling gear. Apparently, some guests have signed up for the gear in advance and he's checking their names off on a clipboard.

Real old school.

When everyone has their gear, I climb down from the rock and approach him.

I eyeball his name tag first. "Sheldon, I was wondering if you have any extra snorkeling gear I could use."

"No, sorry. We only brought them for the guests who said they wanted to use them. Most people bring their own."

At my disappointed look, he bites his bottom lip and tilts his head. "You can use Keston's gear. But you said you're not his girl. So . . . I don't know."

I glance around for the bartender. I find him hanging out by the large cooler, eating a plate of food, and holding court with his fans.

"Yeah, sure," I smile. "I'm his girl. He won't mind if I use it."

"Cool. Well, you're not on the list," he holds up the clipboard, "so just bring it back when you're done."

"I will, thanks."

He climbs back onto the boat and brings me some nice snorkeling gear. Better than the ones they're giving the guests.

No way am I coming all this way to this bucket list destination, known for its pristine reefs and superb snorkeling, and *not* get in the water. If Keston can pretend to be a therapist, I can pretend to be his girl.

I forgo the large flippers and slip the snorkeling mask over my curly hair. It's one of those new ones that covers my full face and doesn't get tangled up in my hair.

Feeling very Jacques Cousteau, I step into the shimmering blue-green water and duck under. I immediately feel as if I've passed through a portal into a magical realm.

# Chapter Twenty

Everything I read and saw about No Man's Land is true. None of it was hype. This is the real deal.

Gentle waves lap over my head as I part the water with my arms. Bubbles escape my breathing tube. I hover over large rocks covered in green, blue and purple coral.

It's all so beautiful I want to cry.

No one can talk to me down here. They can't reject me. They can't hurt me.

Not with rainbow fish flickering by, their iridescent colors outshining my swimsuit. All that noise in the world above feels irrelevant down here.

I can feel my heart smiling.

Is this why Keston Kips is always joyful? He gets to exist in this alternate universe.

Then I see it.

A small bobblehead moving up and down. Short paddle feet, and a black shell painted with bright yellow designs.

Oh my goodness. It's looking at me.

I stop moving my feet and arms and just hover like a mermaid. My black curly hair fans around my face.

What does it think of me?

It doesn't. Whoosh! It dives downward and disappears fast.

I thought you turtles were supposed to be slow. Maybe that's just on land. Like us people.

My heart smiles wider.

I swim and swim and swim, breathing in my tube, not bothering to come up for air. Who needs the outside world when you have this perfect space.

A world of fuchsia fish, wavy sea fans, and endless bubbles as the sea smacks nearby rocks.

I wish I had someone special to share it with. Someone who'd get me. Not just the lawyer me. Or the New York me. Or even the quiet me who loves to read while snuggling under a blanket.

But the woman who believes in love and loyalty. Who wants a home and a family. I want to bake cookies and cupcakes for my kids. Snorkel with them and point out the cool marine life.

I want to walk along the shore holding hands with *my* person. Kiss him under a full moon. Sing together under the stars. Play board games as a family when the rain dances on the roof.

It sounds corny, but I want to be the star of my own romantic movie. Where the girl falls in love and the guy loves her back the same. Is that too much to ask?

I shake my head as tears form. This is not a place to cry, CJ. There's more than enough salt water around.

A long silver fish with sharp teeth flashes by my mask.

I blink.

Is that a barracuda? It's as big as my arm. Worry zings through me. How far have I swum?

My head bobs out of the water. My feet swizzle back and forth to keep my head up.

Where's the boat?

A slow panic spreads through me.

I turn this way, and that. Feet kicking hard to stay afloat.

I squint. I can see the white boat hull in the distance. It's close to the strip of sand but moving away from it. Where are they going without me?

I wave my hand in the air. I shake my face mask high. I shout. "Stop!"

Please let someone see me.

I don't want to star in a movie where the captain forgets you in the ocean and you get eaten by a shark.

Oh God. How is this happening to me? Didn't anyone notice I wasn't on board? Didn't anyone care?

I strike out kicking my feet hard, swimming above water, the mask pushed up.

This is what happens to single people. I'm huffing and puffing while kicking like a maniac. If you don't have a partner, you get left behind.

I struggle to stay calm as I fight the rise and fall of the current that thinks nothing of slapping a few waves in my face.

I choke on seawater.

Concentrate CJ. Take a deep breath out of the water. Not under it.

Salt burns my eyes. Is it the seawater? Or the forbidden tears?

I'm still far away from the beach. I realize why it was so easy to swim out here. The current was carrying me along.

Now, the current is pushing me backward. For my every two strokes forward the current laughs and pushes me backward. The sea is playing a game with me. A very dangerous game.

# Chapter Twenty-One

There are moments when my limbs are so heavy with exhaustion that I want to give up this push-pull fight. Like seriously. I never imagined I'd ever want to give up. But I experience a few moments of pure despair. And it ain't pretty.

"You're not dying here, CJ." I shout at myself in my head.

I've given up hope of reaching the sailboat. I'm focusing on the beach. The white sand and coconut trees. Straight ahead.

I throw one arm forward and drag water in my cupped palm, then another arm forward. Repeat, repeat, repeat. My leg muscles are burning up, but I kick and kick. My lungs feel like they will explode. But if I stop, I swallow water making my throat burn with the salt.

I hear my spin class instructor shouting in my head, "Pedal, pedal, pedal." I close my eyes and do that. Pedal my legs like I'm pedaling all the way to shore. Like I'm pedaling to *Wanna be startin' somethin'* by Michael Jackson, the song she played the most in class.

Giselle forced me to go to those classes. If it weren't for her, I'd have drowned already.

The world that seemed so beautiful and peaceful and magical has transformed into a living nightmare. Kind of how life can turn on you.

I'm still halfway to the shore. The trees look like popsicles waving in the breeze. The rocks resemble dragons with hunched backs. Am I hallucinating? A splash near me throws water in my face.

I wipe my eyes. It's the turtle. He's swimming next to me.

I'm not hallucinating. His little head swivels and I swear he looks directly at me. His mouth opens and closes. Is he trying to tell me something? He nods his head. I swear he's telling me I can do this. No one will ever believe this.

The turtle nods its diamond-shaped head once more then deep dives beneath me.

"Don't leave me," I cry.

The sun pours its golden rays on my tangled curls burning my scalp as if to make sure I know nature is stronger than I can ever be.

I search my mind for something to hold on to. I'm a New

Yorker. New Yorkers survive all kinds of hell. The A train on a Monday morning is a ride through damnation.

As the sun and the sea burn my body, my mind sharpens on a thought.

I'm a Black woman born in America. I wouldn't exist if it weren't for my strong ass ancestors surviving the Middle Passage. Surviving this very sea that's trying to take me down now.

No fucking way! I can't let them down.

I kick my legs with renewed energy. I channel my ancestors and ride the waves on their spirits. Because I can't die out here.

# Chapter Twenty-Two

**B**ut even my ancestors' spirits can't ferry me across the ocean forever.

I feel my body sinking below the surface. There's not one ounce of strength left in me to fight.

That's when a shadow blocks the sun. A strong water spirit wraps its tentacles around my waist and drags me somewhere.

To the bottom of the sea? To the pearly gates?

I close my eyes. Heavenly peace. I feel nothing at all. No more achy lungs. No more burning legs. No more anything. I'm being transported across the water, my lungs squashed by the unyielding tentacles.

My head falls back on something warm. I'm gazing upward at the blue cloudless sky.

Is this heaven? If so, why is my skin itching? And my throat aflame with a thousand fire ants.

I groan and cough.

"Easy," a sing-song voice says.

God is an islander?

Bile fills my throat. I turn my face and vomit. It stings so bad.

What is happening to me? I thrash my arms and feel soft grainy sand. Am I dreaming?

God hears my silent questions. "No, you're not dreaming."

"Argh," I groan. "Make this stop please." My entire body feels as if it's moving with the waves. Rocking back and forth on a never-ending carnival ride.

I think I pass out. When I open my eyes again, I'm lying under the shade of a coconut tree. The pain shooting through my body has eased a tiny bit.

I curl into a fetal position. "I want to go home," I cry. But no sound comes out of my dry scratchy throat.

I can only stare at the hallucination before me.

A man is slashing down palm branches with his bare hands. He's piling them in a big heap. He rests one arm high against the tree trunk and leans forward, wiping sweat from his brow with his other hand. In my deranged mind, I think he's one of those romance book heroes come to life.

He must feel my stare because he looks over.

When he sees me, I give a tiny wave with two fingers. It's the best I can do under the circumstances. You know, the near-death, almost drowned circumstances.

He hurries over, a grim expression on his face.

His knees hit the sand. He growls, "What the hell were you doing swimming so far out, woman? You could have died. You would have died if I didn't get here in time." He spits out the last word as if it hurts him.

But why would it?

Did I make Keston Kips lose his happy-go-lucky persona?

Is he actually mad? At me?

"I'm sorry," I squeak out. "When is the boat coming back?"

# Chapter Twenty-Three

The secret to being great at anything is preparation. We heard it often in law school. I learned it firsthand in the courtroom from irate judges who accused me of not being prepared for every situation (like an unscheduled settlement for three million dollars and what do I mean I don't have the approval of my client?).

After fifteen years of being a lawyer, I can tell you without hesitation that I am *always* prepared. Which means I'm ready for any and everything.

But when Keston Kips looks me dead in the eye, not a smirk in sight, and says in a dire voice, "There isn't another boat for days," I am floored. Well, technically, *sanded*.

My mouth opens and closes more than once as my brain scrambles to process that information.

I push myself up and lean back against the coconut tree. I'm not sure how I got here, or even how I got out of that backstabbing pretty sea, (I assume it was my gallant hero here), but I need to focus on the immediate issue.

I switch from invalid to interrogator at the drop of a coconut.

"Our boat isn't coming back for us?"

He shakes his head.

"Why not? Didn't they see you get off?"

He shakes his head again.

I frown. His bronzed face glows with the exertion of decimating a bunch of coconut branches.

Focus CJ, who cares about Keston Kips' sharp cheekbones, square jaw, and piercing dark eyes? Or his . . .

"Are you okay?"

I shake my head hard. "Water in my ears. I hear a buzzing sound."

Keston snatches something out of the air. "It's a mosquito." He opens his palm. A dead insect falls out.

"Ugh," I shiver.

He rolls his eyes. "As I was saying . . . there's no boat coming for us. Not today anyway. And no one saw me dive off the boat and swim toward you."

"You saved me?"

This time he nods. "I did." His voice is solemn.

I glance up from under my eyelashes. "I owe you."

"You could just say thanks."

"Thanks."

"Okay. Don't make me regret it."

"I won't," I promise. "But let's be real. We can call the resort, right? They'll send another boat for us?"

Keston takes his phone out of his pocket and shakes his head sorrowfully. "Useless. It got wet when I dove in."

"Where's my bag? I left my phone in it. I have a waterproof case. And international data."

I couldn't send a picture earlier. Maybe I can send a regular word text though.

"I had no idea you had a bag on the beach. I didn't see one."

I scramble upwards but my knees buckle. I sink back down.

"Take it easy. You've been through a lot. Tell me where it is."

I point to the rocks where I was sitting earlier. "Before I went snorkeling, I hid my beach bag carefully. Like any New Yorker would."

"Where?"

"Walk past the highest rock, then take a left. Walk past two more rocks then take a right. It's in a crevice."

He narrows his eyes at me. "What's in the bag? Gold?"

I smack my arm where a mosquito tries to take a lunch break. "Hurry up, please. My bug spray is in it."

Keston heads off on his mission to locate my beach bag.

Meanwhile, I assess my body. Other than the ache in my arms and legs, and my still scratchy throat, I feel fine.

My skin doesn't look so good. Salt residue has left white marks. Mosquitoes have left red splotches.

I'm in need of a nice, warm, scented bath, some rich body lotion, and a good face scrub. I can't wait to get back to my villa and put this almost disastrous day behind me.

"Found it!" Keston loops back looking like a golden retriever with a prize.

"Thank you," I say graciously, although I want to snatch it from his hands.

I open it up to find my phone. Thank God, it still has some charge. I check to make sure cellular data is on. Then dust off my fingers and type out a text message. I copy and paste it to two recipients.

One for the resort and one for Giselle.

"Help! I am stuck with a Cocoa Reef employee on No Man's Land. Please send a boat for us before it gets too late. Thanks."

I inhale deeply. Press send on both and wait. Please iPhone, don't fail me now.

# Chapter Twenty-Four

"It's not working!" I cry, staring at the little red exclamation mark and the words, "Not Delivered."

Keston sits back on his heels. His silence is not making me feel better. Where is the happy-go-lucky dude when I need him?

"Let me try," he says.

I give him the phone. He walks up and down the beach holding it high. He climbs rocks with it. He even climbs the coconut tree to find a signal.

I'm so fascinated as he shimmies upwards, his strong muscled thighs gripping the trunk, I forget to be worried.

"Any luck?" I ask when he returns to my side.

"Sorry." He hands me the phone. "Turn it off to save the battery."

I try calling the resort first, but that doesn't work either.

"What does this mean?"

He spreads his hands open. "We're stuck here."

"Noooooo!" I wail. "Someone has to notice we're not on board the boat and come back for us."

He points at the evening sky which is putting on a show of colors. "It's too late for the boat to come back. Even if they notice we're not on board. I can tell you for a fact, no one will know I'm not there. The crew handles the coolers when we dock. And you aren't even on the passenger list."

"What about the women?"

"What women?"

"Oh. My. God! Are you dense? All those women who were dancing . . . or trying to dance with you. They're going to be looking for you right?"

For once I'm hoping his charm will come in handy.

"Nope. I told them to leave me alone."

"You did what? Why!?"

He shrugs.

I drop my head in my hands. "I can't spend the night here. I can't. I'm not prepared for this."

I unfold my designer cover-up and slip it on, pulling it all the way down while still seated. "I don't have any clothes. Or toiletries. Or . . ." I look around wildly. "A bed!" I hear the pitiful wail in my voice, and *I* feel sorry for myself.

"Keston Kips, you have to think of something!"

"What do you want me to do?"

I grind my teeth. "Why do I have to think of everything?"

He gives me a look that says, *careful*. "We're only stuck here because you wanted to go play the little mermaid."

I swallow any more fighting words that could alienate my only comrade.

I search my brain. "Can't we light a fire to get someone's attention? Let people know we're stuck here?"

"This isn't *Pirates of the Caribbean*! I'm not Johnny Depp. You're not Keira Knightley. Plus no one on St. Nick can see a fire from this beach."

"You've got to have ideas. This is your island. What're we going to do?"

"We'll have to make the best of it."

"What does that mean?"

He raises up his hands. "It means we find a way to get comfortable. It'll be a while before we're rescued."

"Define awhile."

"Tuesday."

"What?! Today is Friday. Tuesday is," I hold up a hand with four fingers pointing up, "four whole days away. We could die here."

"She can count."

I frown. "This is no time for sarcasm."

"Or for insults."

I ignore that. "Why on Tuesday? Why not tomorrow?"

"The boat doesn't come every day. Tuesday is the next time we can expect it."

"Well, won't your boss and co-workers realize you're missing from work and raise the alarm?"

He chuckles. "One, I'm not missing from work. I'm done for today. Two, I took the weekend off, from Friday to Monday. For personal reasons. I'm not expected back at work until Tuesday. Three, even if I were missing, no one would raise any alarms. I'm not *five*."

"Well, the personal reason will notice you're missing right?"

He smirks. "You're the personal reason. I took the weekend off because I wanted to take you on an island tour on my bike. Show you the local spots."

I stare at him. "You took a whole weekend off for *me*?"

That sounds so extravagant. Marcus wouldn't do that until he knew me for years. Actually . . . I don't know if Marcus would ever do that.

He sighs. "You seemed sad and lonely. I wanted to cheer you up."

"Oh my, a pity tour. I'm an independent woman. I can go on my own tour. Just because I broke up with my boyfriend . . ."

"Of five years," he says wearily. "I know."

I stop. "Five years is a long time to commit to someone."

"Well, we'll only have four days."

"Thank God for that."

Although what am I saying? I don't want any days. I want off this island.

I get up and stretch out my legs. I shake off any remaining pain, which seems more in my mind now anyway. Like that swim is a bad memory I must bury to focus on the current situation.

"What about you?" he asks, standing up and giving me an arm to lean on. "Won't anyone at the front desk or housekeeping notice *you're* missing?"

I shrug away his arm. "No."

"Why not? Our hotel staff is very attentive. They check on the guests. It's their job."

"I told everyone I didn't want to do any activities and not to call and check on me."

"Woman, you must make friends! You never know when you'll need a helping hand in life."

"Is that your quote of the day?"

"It's my quote for life. St. Nicholas is a small island. We help each other. With everything."

"Oh."

Loud noises rumble from my stomach. I clasp a hand to my midsection.

He raises an eyebrow.

"You should have eaten more than that tiny piece of lobster. No one diets on vacation."

His smug look irritates me.

"I'm not on a diet. I watch what I eat. I'm extremely . . ."

"Picky?"

"I was going to say, discerning."

"Oh," he looks at me closely. "You thought I wouldn't know what that word means, didn't you?"

I have enough shame not to answer that.

He shakes his head. "Okay, Ms. Discerning. I guess you'll be going hungry for the next four days. You should fill up at every meal. In case of emergencies like this."

"That's mean. But fine. It'll be like fasting. I can do that for a few days." My stomach growls in disagreement. *Feed me*, it seems to be shouting. *Feed me now!*

He rubs his non-existent belly. "Glad I had seconds of that potato salad and macaroni pie and . . ."

"I get it." I look around in an attempt to bring the subject away from food. "Where are we going to sleep?"

Just then a dark bird flies out of a tree and circles my head.

"Ahh! What kind of bird is that?" Another one flies by and then another. "There's lots of them here."

"Those aren't birds. They're bats."

*"Ahhhhhh!"* My piercing scream scares away two oncoming bats from circling my head. I wave my arms around like windmills. This is too much. No boat, no food, no fresh water, no place to sleep, and now bats?

Hot tears prick at my eyes. "I can't take any more disasters."

Strong, warm arms encircle my shoulders. "It's going to be okay. Bats eat mosquitoes and other insects. They don't attack humans. They just have a bad rep from vampire and Batman movies."

"But what about rabies?" I sniffle, leaning closer to his warm body.

"If you don't attack them, they won't attack you."

"Sounds like another quote of the day."

"I'm using them up for real. Got to save some for tomorrow. Let's get away from these trees. The bats seem to be living somewhere up there."

I hop across the sand putting distance between myself and the tree bats.

As we reach the tongue of sand that sticks out into the sea, something silver splashes in the water.

"What's that? Better not be a shark."

Keston shifts his gaze from my face to the sea on his right side. A school of small silvery fish rise in an arc over the water and splash back down.

"I've never seen anything like that. They were so in sync."

Keston turns back to me, eyes alight with excitement.

"You hungry?"

"Duh."

"Let's go fishing!"

"With what? How?"

I don't want to admit that I'm a forty-year-old woman who's never been fishing in her life.

Hand to jaw, Keston studies the beach. "Those are called grunts," he says, scanning the shoreline. "Tiny fish. If we had a net, we could catch a bunch and cook them on the leftover embers from the beach BBQ. They're delicious."

"But we don't have a net."

His gaze lands on me. He lifts a hem of my gorgeous sparkly beach cover up.

"It's Versace."

"Uh-huh."

He'd better get his sandy fingers off my designer wear.

"What're you doing?"

He fingers the hem, looks at the water, then back at me.

"Do you trust me?"

"No," I shake my head vigorously.

He responds with his devil-may-care grin. "You should. I'm about to get us dinner, honey."

"Don't call me honey."

"Sorry, sugar."

I roll my eyes. My stomach rolls, too.

"Lend me your dress."

"What?"

"It's perfect. We'll swoop in and catch a bunch of grunts with this thing."

"This thing must have cost almost one thousand U.S. dollars."

He whistles. "This is gonna be one expensive dinner then. Not to mention you could have bought a new paddle board for the price of this flimsy material." He shakes his head.

"Don't you have anything else you can use?" It's my turn to look around frantically.

Another big splash comes from the shallow water.

"We'll miss our chance if we don't move now. Fish aren't going to be jumping for long."

"Fine," I grouse. "Here!" I can't believe I'm giving him my birthday present. I pull it over my head and stand before him in my tiny, blue-green bikini.

"Nice," he grins.

"Just get us some fish."

He raises his arms and yanks his t-shirt over his head, tossing it on the sand. I wasn't expecting him to do that.

Two curved muscular dips of flesh and bone snake down into his board shorts.

I gulp.

You could tell his physique is all natural. It doesn't look like he lifts weights or works out, unless you call serving drinks, dancing salsa, and playing beach volleyball with the guests "working out."

"Uh CJ, are you ready?"

I raise my head. He's staring at me staring at him. Damn. How obvious can I be? He'll think I'm a lovestruck teenager. It's not as if I like this dude. He just looks good.

"Ready for what?"

He winks and walks into the sea. "To catch our dinner, of course."

"Me, too?"

He nods slowly like I'm lacking in intelligence, which I am where this whole "fishing with my beach dress" is concerned.

Or any fishing, actually.

I'm so out of my element, it isn't even funny.

I follow him into the sea. It's really the last place I want to be after the ocean had its way with me earlier.

But the warm water does feel nice on my sore calves. I follow Keston in up to my waist. This clear blue water is deceptive.

"I'm not ready to forgive you for seducing me, and then trying to drag me to my death," I murmur to the sea.

"Are you talking to the water?"

"Maybe," I shrug. "We have some unfinished business."

"Well, let's focus on *this* business. I need your help."

For the first time since getting stuck, I smile. "Okay."

I can do this. I can fish for my dinner. I'm not a total diva. I'll show this dude I'm more than expensive clothes and fancy drinks.

A silvery cloud of fast-moving fish jump near my shoulders. I let out a piercing squeal.

"Shhh, you'll scare them away." His rakish smile is back.

Does he ever stop with that charm? It's not going to work out here.

"You're doing great, though. I'm proud of you," he adds.

For some reason, his words relax me. I even preen myself a bit. Although all I've done so far is walk into the water.

"Catch." He unexpectedly throws my beach dress into the air. I gasp. It's going to get wet.

I reach up and grab one side as he grabs the other side of the sparkly netted dress on its way down. I follow his lead, bending my knees into the sea and scooping the dress downwards under the water, then quickly yanking it back up.

"*Ahhhhh!*" This time my scream could shake the bats right out of the trees.

Tiny, silver fish are darting about in my Versace dress. They're hundreds of them. Thousands. And so disorganized. Some swimming this way, some that way, as the water drains through the tiny holes of my cover-up until only the little fish remain.

"Damn, woman, you're good at this. You sure you haven't done this before? I can't believe you got it on the first try."

I look away so I won't have to see the fish muddling around in my once-beloved dress. "Let's just get them out of here." I grit my teeth and walk toward the beach. Keston follows with his end of the dress.

"This better be delicious," I mutter under my breath.

"Oh, it will be, princess. It will be."

# Chapter Twenty-Six

I watch as Keston stirs up the coconut husks and coals, relights the fire with a lighter he carries in his dry bag, and sets about grilling the batch of small fish on the lobster grill they'd used earlier for the beach BBQ.

While the fish is grilling, he disappears into the jungle. He returns a half hour later with a stalk of miniature bananas and a bottle.

"Oh my God, are those real bananas?"

He drops the treasure at my feet. He yanks one out of the bunch and peels away the bright yellow skin.

"Here, try it."

I don't waste a moment. I take the offered fruit and eat it in two big bites.

I wipe my mouth with the back of my hand.

"Where'd you get this bunch of bananas?"

"They grow wild all around."

"Cool. May I have another one?"

He peels three more small bananas and hands them to me one by one. I eat each one pushing all thoughts of carbs out of my head. This is a freaking emergency.

"Look what else I found?"

I peer at the silver bottle in his hand. "Rum? Did you find rum on No Man's Land? Who are you, Johnny Depp?"

He smirks. Just like Johnny. "It's an emergency stash the boat crew leaves behind. For making rum punch for the guests. I think this is the last bottle, but I didn't look hard. There could be more." He pours out a capful and takes a swig. Makes a face and smiles.

"Here." He pours another capful. "It's 150 proof, made with my island's sugar cane, and sold in the stores."

I push his hand away, spilling a few drops.

"Watch it woman, this is a precious commodity."

"For you maybe. I need lime and coconut and a cute umbrella with my rum."

"I might be able to arrange that." He eyes the surrounding coconut trees.

"I was kidding."

"I'm not."

Keston buries the rum bottle in cool sand next to my coconut tree, Prince Harry, and tends to the tiny fish.

When the fish are ready, he prepares two large banana leaves, each with a pile of grilled grunts circled with banana slices.

I carry my leaf plate carefully to sit on a coconut tree stump. "Nice presentation."

"Thanks. I heard Americans prefer to look at their food rather than eat it."

"Oh, yeah?" I scoff. "Watch me."

I don't think I've ever had a better seafood dinner. It's like eating a gourmet tin of sardines, except on a beach, smelling of salty air and coconut oil. I could devour two more servings.

The best part is that after we eat, we throw our leaf plates onto the fire.

"Thank you," I tell Keston. "It was great. A keto diet it is."

"I don't know what a keto is, but I have dessert."

He digs around in his dry bag and pulls out a squishy bag of M&M's. He shakes his candy like it's a bag of coins.

"You carry M&M's around? Don't they melt in the heat?"

"Nope. They never last long enough to melt. I'm an M&M monster."

"I can't recall the last time I ate this kind of candy. I prefer dark Swiss or pure Ecuadorian chocolate."

"*Oh la la,*" he says, tossing some into his mouth.

Maybe it's because night is advancing, or because the fish dinner was so yummy . . . or because I feel tired and weirdly relaxed, but I stick out my palm. "I'll have a couple."

I nibble slowly on the edges of my tiny chocolate circles.

"Don't you think we should ration our food?" I ask as Keston throws M&M's up in the air and catches them expertly in his mouth.

He laughs. "Why?"

Damn, he's so careless. "It's what people stuck on desert islands do."

"You mean on reality shows?"

"And in movies and books."

"You worry too much."

"And you not at all. Must be what they call *island* living."

He smiles lazily. "It's just called *living* here."

Ugh. He irritates me so much. Is it irrational to worry about our food? I bet he hasn't even considered where we'll sleep. And the sun has almost slipped away completely. Dusk is fast turning to night. The bats will return and who knows what else flies around out here.

I shiver in my bikini and move closer to the fire. My beach cover-up is almost dry. Unfortunately, I must wear it again . . . until the next time we go fishing.

I stare into the flames. Marcus O'Brien and his luxury *everything* is so tempting. If I could contact him, I bet he'd send a helicopter for me. But I've cut those ties. Deleted his numbers. Not to mention, I have no service.

My head plops down on my hand. I'm seriously stuck on an island with a man I barely know. For four days. This is not a vacation. It's a nightmare.

# Chapter Twenty-Seven

"Never have I ever thought I'd be stuck on a deserted island." This thought is spinning around in my head as I use my phone light to walk down the beach looking for a personal bush to squat behind and relieve myself.

"You're wasting our light," Keston shouts. "No need to walk so far away in the dark. It's not as if I can *see* you."

As I perform a semi-crow pose from yoga class so there'd be no splashing on my feet, I think about all the things I would have brought with me in my oversized beach bag if I knew this could or would occur.

A flashlight, snacks, toilet paper, a satellite phone, and a huge bottle of Advil. I promise never to leave home without a satellite phone ever again. Even on the subway.

I stroll back down the beach under the light of the moon, the waves lapping at my feet. I can't imagine the New York subway. It's as if I've entered an alternate dimension. One where civilization does not exist. It's just me and this bartender, who is annoying but useful.

He actually built a cute, if not exactly sturdy, place to sleep. An authentic tiki hut out of the stack of palm branches he'd decimated on the beach earlier.

While Keston was doing his Frank Lloyd Wright impersonation, making our tiki hut evolve from the environment of sand and stone, I performed one of my daily rituals.

My yoga instructor insists that no matter where we are, we should find time for ourselves on our mats.

I don't have a mat. But I have the entire stretch of sand.

With Keston working on our "house" I stretched my arms high then pretzeled into downward dogs, planks, cats and cows, and pigeons. She'd be proud of me.

Normally I follow yoga by writing three things I'm grateful for in my gratitude journal. But ever since my breakup with Marcus, the journal has fallen by the wayside. I didn't even bring it to St. Nick's.

Upon my return from my "bathroom," I sit down in the tiki hut and help Keston braid strips of palm branches together to make sleeping mats.

"Never have I ever made my own bed out of coconut tree branches," I say.

Keston hums as his hands work speedily. I watch him twisting and braiding his strips of palm while I fiddle with the slippery suckers that unravel as quickly as I twine them.

"Damn, you've done this before."

He nods, biting a strip of palm and ripping it in two.

"I'm not putting that in my mouth."

He spits out the floppy palm strip from between his teeth. "Pretend you're braiding your hair."

I sniff. "I go to a salon for that."

"Of course you do. Okay, pretend you're braiding your daughter's hair."

I feel as if I've been gut-punched. "Shut up."

He raises puzzled eyes to me. "What's wrong?"

I swear under my breath. Bad words I save for bad moments.

"Not one *fucking* thing, okay."

He holds up both his hands. "I hit a nerve. Sorry."

I get up and flounce out of the little shelter. "You hit a lot of nerves," I shout. "All you hit are nerves."

I wrap my arms around my body to stop the shaking.

The moon shines its blue-white light down on me in a mocking stare. Like it knows how I'm feeling, even if I'm not sure what pain this is coursing through my veins.

I feel rather than hear footsteps behind me. Keston's voice is soft. "Hey, it'll be okay. We'll get rescued. Think of this as a mini adventure. Like a . . . nature retreat."

"I used to want to escape to a private island," I say in muffled tones. "I never thought it would come true."

"There you go. This is your fantasy come to life."

I snort, wiping away invisible tears. "And what are you?"

"Girl, I can be anything you want me to be."

I turn around and swat his arm. "You know you don't have to use the bartender spiel on me. It's disgusting. And unnecessary. And you have my undivided attention." I throw up my arms. "It's not as if I have anyone else to talk to."

The grin on his face could charm the devil himself. "That 'spiel'—he air quotes the word—got you to bounce back from whatever black hole you were dropping into. Look at you. Scolding me like a pro."

My hands find my hips and I sway my body weight to one foot. "Don't make me smack you again."

His eyes light up. A sexy smile snakes across his firm lips. "If that works for you. I'm in."

My heart skips a beat. I eye him skeptically.

"Is that a come-on?"

He shrugs, drawing a line in the sand with his big toe.

Did I mention he has the most beautiful feet?

"Do you get pedicures?" I blurt, eyeing his perfectly crescent-shaped toenails.

His laugh is sweet and musical. Like steel pans in the night air. "Do I get pedicures? *Hahahaha.*"

He captures one of my arms and nestles it under his. "Let's finish making our beds and we can discuss it." His voice is smooth and gentle. Like he's encouraging a baby bird to fly.

I'm the baby bird in this scenario.

# Chapter Twenty-Eight

Dinner. Check.
 Shelter. Check.
 Sleeping mats. Check.
Bathroom spot. Check.
My brain and body are exhausted. I can't wait to flop down on my pallet. But I'm worried.

"We need to prepare for tomorrow." I'm leaning on the walking stick Keston made for me. It's also a stylus and is now being used to write a "To do" list on the sand.

Keston eyes my sand tablet with confusion.

"Why are you writing things we already did? Isn't a *to do* list for reminding you what you must do *in the future*?"

"It's good to write down your accomplishments."

"Why? They're in the past."

I blink.

"You're patting yourself on the back for finding a pee spot?" he asks, brows furrowed.

I glare at him.

Does this man not realize the importance of documenting achievements?

"Anyway, can we go to sleep?" he says. "Let tomorrow take care of itself."

I double blink. "No. That's not how it works. We must write down what we have to do. Like find some fresh water!" My voice rises on a loud squeal of fear.

He waves a hand in the air in a cavalier manner.

"We haven't even thought about what we'll drink when our water bottles run empty," I point out.

I'd been rationing sips on my secret bottle of Perrier while sharing my regular bottled water with him.

"It'll be fine," he says.

"I'm not drinking my pee," I continue as he stares dumbfounded at me. "I don't care if I have to be thirsty until Tuesday."

He shakes his head as he slides his leanly muscled torso down onto a mat. "You're a psycho. But I like you."

"It's offensive to call someone a psycho."

He leans toward me. "I agree. I won't call someone that. Just you."

I toss the stick down and suck my teeth hard. "You are an awful person. You need to get your toxic masculinity in check."

"It's my masculinity that built this shelter, thank you very much."

I sniff hard. "That's exactly what a toxic male would say."

"I'll build you your own tiki hut as you call it. And find us fresh water. Now let's get some sleep. We have a lot to do tomorrow."

I perk up. "Like what?"

I itch to grab my stick and start writing in the sand again. Doesn't he realize the older you get the more forgetful? I can barely remember what I wore yesterday, much less a list of stuff to do tomorrow.

No answer. Gentle snores escape his lips. I crawl as close to him as I can without touching his body. It's probably uncomfortable. All those hard angles and planes. Those bulging humps and bumps.

As if reading my mind, Keston's large hand crooks around me and pats my head. In a second, it's gone. "Night, CJ."

"Good night." But I can't sleep. I fidget this way and that. My skin is covered with mosquito repellant. My dress is itchy after being used as a net. My mind is racing with worse-case scenarios.

Mostly though, I can't sleep because I don't know whether to snuggle closer or pull away from this man who must think this is Neverland and I'm Wendy to his Peter Pan.

"It's okay to sleep with the enemy," he says softly.

"I won't respond to that."

I stare at the palms above my head rustling in the island breeze. Are any lizards nesting there? Will they drop on me while I'm sleeping? I shiver and move closer.

"Here." Keston hands me a flower in the dark. Its white petals glow under the moonlight shining through the branches.

He must have picked it before coming inside. I press my face to the lovely white petals.

"Oh wow, this is gorgeous." I inhale the scented flower again. "It's intoxicating."

"Night-blooming jasmine flowers. Remind me to tell you the story of the princess who fell in love with the Sun."

"Okay," I say, drifting off to sleep, my flower tucked under my chin. My back to Keston Kips' back. It feels like the safest haven I'll find out here. Might as well make the most of it.

"I'd kill for a shower," I mutter before my eyelids close.

# Chapter Twenty-Nine

I really feel my age when I can't move my neck the next morning.

At twenty-three, I could have slept outside on a beach, a few palm branches for cushions, and leaped up to greet the day.

Maybe I could have done it at thirty, or even thirty-five. But something happens when you hit thirty-eight. And forget about forty.

Creature comforts become a thing. Like a BIG thing. You have your favorite fork. Favorite bowl. You love and adore your espresso machine to the point that you buy a mini one to take on trips. Your pillow becomes your best friend and it might as well have its own passport.

Most importantly, you sit in the same spot, with the same placemat at your kitchen table. Every time you eat.

Which is why, my waking up on hard sand, a crick in my neck and an ache in my side, no espresso machine in sight, or pillow to hug, I want to bawl. I glance over carefully at Keston's side of the hut. His palm fronds are smooshed flat, but he's gone.

I crawl slowly and painfully out of the tiki hut to find that the sun is already beaming hard in the cloudless sky. I check my phone. It's only eight o'clock. I turn the phone back off to save my battery.

"Hello?" I try to call out from my parched throat.

I take a tiny sip of water. Then a second sip. When I get back to civilization, I'll remember to be grateful for a fridge and cold water.

I walk down the beach to my personal "bathroom" area. After handling my business and washing up with salt water, I go in search of Keston.

I can imagine the crazy mess I must be. My hair is springy and fluffing all around my face. My skin is scratched and ashy. My face . . . forget my face. I refuse to look in a mirror. With no Keston Kips in sight after a walk up and down the curved shoreline, I collapse under a shady tree and search my beach bag for anything edible.

"I can't believe it's only Saturday," I tell the coconut tree, as

I pull out the Kennedy Ryan novel. The bug spray and sunblock. And a headband. Oh yeah!

I tie it around my curls immediately.

Then halleluiah. A granola bar. I remember grabbing it from the breakfast table yesterday. It seems so long ago.

I rip the shiny paper off the thin bar with my teeth and take a bite. God. This is the *best* granola bar.

After another bite, I feel a stab of guilt and wrap up the remainder to share with Keston. It's bad enough I didn't share my Perrier water.

"Can you believe I have to live like this for two more days?!"

The tree waves its branches over my head.

I cock an eyebrow at the trunk. "You don't think I'll survive, do you? Thanks a lot."

"Well, I see one of us has already gone mad," Keston walks out of the dark tangle of trees looking like Brendan Fraser in *The Mummy*—all rugged, sweaty, and hot.

"I was having a private conversation with Prince Harry." I pat the tree trunk. "He's quite the pessimist."

"Why do you call it Prince Harry?"

I look upwards. "It was the first thing that came to mind when I saw it standing tall, all regal with red/orange fronds. The other trees lean and sway. This one is a stand up guy. *Tree.*"

He nods, like he accepts that wacky explanation. "Excuse me for interrupting your one-on-one with the prince. I have good news and I have bad news."

"Noooo," I groan like a teenager. "I can't take any bad news."

"It's not soooo bad," he says, also sounding like a teen.

Oh great. We're reverting to children and soon we'll be all *Lord of the Flies* up in here.

I shiver at the thought.

"Give me the good news. Save the bad for another time."

He leans an arm against the tree, crosses one foot over the other, and stares down at me as if he owns the island. "You have to say, please."

I roll my eyes. "Please. Your majesty."

"Just a simple please would have been fine. You know for an older woman you sure act like a spoiled girl."

I slap a mosquito away. He's right. I am acting like a brat. And it's my fault he's stuck here. Plus, he saved my life. I should be a little grateful to him.

I hug the tree trunk as I stand up. Not because I think I'll look like a pole dancer. But because I need the help getting up.

Keston is still in his bad boy lean. I look him in the eye. In the humblest voice I can manage I say, "Please give me the good news. I need to hear some."

That slow, sexy, butter-melting grin appears.

"Put on your flip flops and come with me." He takes my hand and steps toward the dark woods that lead away from the beach and into the interior of the island. A place I hoped I wouldn't have to go. Not with all those bats in there.

He feels my hesitation because he tugs my hand gently. "It's okay. You'll like it."

"Says the lion to the mouse," I mutter. I close my eyes and plunge through the thicket of trees, praying the bats are normal nocturnal bats that sleep the day away.

# Chapter Thirty

We walk about thirty minutes through the green jungle. Keston pushes vines apart with his bare hands to clear a path for us to walk. I step carefully over the mossy rocks.

Giant emerald ferns grow wild and free. Leaves the size of my entire body wave their shocking greenness at me.

"It feels as if we'll see fairies in here," I whisper.

He chuckles. "I was thinking I'd wake a sleeping dragon. Or run into a pirate ghost. It's been a long time since I've been in this rainforest. I was about fifteen. Me and four friends came in search of pirate treasure."

"There's pirate treasure in here?" I ask, eyes wide now, staring at the trees as if gold doubloons are hidden amongst their giant roots. It would make this entire misadventure worth it.

"Why did you only come once? Did you find anything?"

He shakes his head. "It was weird. I remember we thought it was haunted."

"Because of all the dead pirates?"

"Maybe."

I hear it before I see it. The loud rush of water. It reminds me of how I discovered the river near the resort. How far away that day seems now. The day Keston apologized with a smooth-as-honey drink that I would kill for now.

We step into a clearing. The sun's rays illuminate a wide pool of clear water surrounded on three sides by walls of rock. A cascade of water flows over the rock through rays of light spraying droplets into the shimmery air. As we walk closer, the spray hits our faces. With all the sea salt I've absorbed, this cascading spray feels like I'm being blessed by a divine presence.

"I could cry with happiness right now." I spread my arms wide. "Look at this place."

Keston beams at me. "I wanted to dive in, but I came to get you first."

"It's like a dreamscape." I point at my body. "I've felt whack since I woke up. This is exactly what I need. I can't wait to go in."

"Please. You look like you belong in the wild. Check out your gorgeous hair." He ruffles my curls.

I grin and shake it wildly about. "I'm going for au natural."

Something about being totally alone on an island makes stuff you usually care about feel unimportant. Like makeup. Which I never leave home without. I have some in my beach bag but haven't even thought about using it.

"I'm taking off my swimsuit and washing it," I say in a challenging voice.

"I sure hope so. I plan on washing my shirt and shorts."

I look at him. "So, we're skinny dipping?"

He arches a brow. "I call it bathing."

"Right."

I watch as he rips his shirt off. His hands reach for the strings on the front of his shorts.

I hesitate. "Should we take off our clothes at the same time?"

He stops undressing. The look he gives me is so gentle and pure. "Sure. But it's not a big deal."

I sigh. "It is for me."

"I can look away if you want. While you slide into the pool."

Do I need to explain that while he works and plays half-naked every day, I feel more comfortable covering up? At least my private parts. I'm not *that* au naturel.

I shake my head. "Let's do it at the same time."

"Okay. On the count of three," he says.

I nod.

As Keston counts, I get more and more nervous. We're crossing a line.

And I'm not twenty years old anymore. I don't have perfect curves and smooth skin like the girl in *Blue Lagoon*.

But that cascading waterfall looks so inviting. I can't wait to stand under it and let the fresh water wash my sticky skin clean.

"Three!" he shouts, dropping his shorts.

"Hold up." I was so busy worrying about being naked that I forgot to untie the knot at my neck. After pulling on it for a second, it's even knottier.

He turns around. Full frontal nudity. I feel like I'm sixteen and seeing my first . . . *package*. For the record, I was eighteen.

What a dweeb I am.

"What?" he asks confidently standing there like a naked Achilles on a rock.

I swallow.

I can't avert my eyes. That would be prudish.

But he's so *all* there! His plush member hangs solid and thick like a grandfather clock pendulum in broad daylight.

I didn't even know God made them that size.

Super-sized.

How old are you? I scold myself. I put on my best lawyer face and focus on the task at hand.

"My string is knotted." I point to the tie around my neck. "Probably the reason I woke up with a crick in my neck."

He jumps from rock to rock to reach me. Everything is swinging loose and let me tell you, it is stunning.

I swallow thickly. "You look very comfortable naked."

"I am. It's normal."

Right. Maybe for you, I think.

Behind me, he tries teasing the knot loose with his fingers. That's not the only thing being teased. A stream of wet heat flows down into my bikini bottoms.

I shake his hands off my neck. "It's okay. I'll go in with my swimsuit on."

"I almost have it." He puts his hot lips against my neck, tugging at the knot.

"What are you doing?" I spin around and find my lady bits pressed up against his thick maleness.

Oh Lord. It's right there. Nothing to stop me from

reaching out and touching it. Stroking it. God, what is wrong with me?

I gulp.

"Do you have to stand so close?" I snap.

He raises both hands. "Sorry. I'm trying to help."

I clench my hands to stop my urge to touch his smooth, brown cockhead.

The stream escalates to a flood. My crease is soaking wet. My pussy has her own mind. I hope he can't feel how damp and ready she is to receive his cock.

He glances at my face which I know is flushed with the heat of anticipation.

My clit contracts with excitement at the thought of this man touching it. I can feel it trembling, pushing its way out from between my folds. It's been so long since it was touched. Stroked. Caressed. Sucked.

God, I bet desire is written all over my face.

"Oh," he smiles lazily. "You want to . . ." His eyes flash downward.

Fuck. He can tell.

I don't wait for him to finish his sentence. I make to push him off the rock I'm standing on. But his hand grabs mine.

"Look, Keston, I'm sorry to disappoint you," I say in a strangled voice. But we're not having sex on this so-called adventure." I hate how my voice is trembling. Like it doesn't agree. Or worse, doesn't believe me.

"Oh, princess. I won't be the one who's disappointed." He gives me a devilish smile, dark eyes gleaming.

I scoff. "I'll take my chances."

To prove my point, I watch him square in his face as I peel my bikini bottoms off, pushing them down one leg then the other, very . . . very . . . slowly.

I don't care that it's damp with my juices. Or that the tell-tale dribble down my legs gives away my secret. His cockiness needs to be reined in. His *cock* needs to be reined in!

When the colorful crochet pile sits in a tiny heap at my feet, I slowly bend over and pick it up, letting it swing from my fingers.

"I can do naked too."

# Chapter Thirty-One

I feel as if I'm watching this scene from somewhere outside my body. I should know better than to play with fire. And Keston Kips is fire. Anyone can see that.

As I swing my bottoms in his face, his eyes darken. They don't leave my face. Yet, I feel as if he's seeing every movement I'm making and taking in every bit of flesh I'm exposing.

We stand there together face to face, eyes daring each other.

He reaches out a long smooth finger. "May I?"

I'm not sure what he's asking permission to do. It's empowering to say the least. To have a man's attention so focused on me. It's something that never happened with Marcus. Not in our whole five years together.

I shrug my shoulders. But I'm anything but indifferent.

He reaches out and slowly runs his finger up the lines and curves of my body. He hovers over the crease of my hip bone.

He slides his finger very slowly across my inner thigh, traveling upwards to the apex of my thighs.

My very bad clit is clenching, pulsating, aching for his finger to stop and stroke her.

His eyes never leave mine as he draws circles around that bundle of nerves. Round and round, stirring my honey pot, but never touching the hood.

My breath inhales sharply as he leaves it and moves upward.

His finger presses firmly on my abdomen, circling my belly button with feathery touches.

All my nerves are on fire.

I feel my eyelids close down.

My breath hitches as his finger travels upward. My two, rose-colored nipples protrude through the holes of my crocheted top.

Lush and full of nerves, they're tightwires straight to my clit.

He presses his finger against one nipple, plucking it like a guitar string over and over. I let out a moan. My knees weaken.

I lean my head back and stare at the sky.

"You are gorgeous." His voice is deep and rough. No more teasing playfulness. No more cockiness.

I can't speak. I'm hypnotized by his finger. It's sliding

between my breasts, lifting my breast up lightly, then moving with purpose toward my other rosy nipple.

Inside, I'm screaming for him to hurry up and touch it.

Squeeze it I want to shout. As he takes his time, hefting up my breast with his finger. Like he's weighing a pound of peas.

I bite my lips and taste blood.

Then finally.

"Oh," I moan. "Don't stop."

He does not disappoint. He slings an arm up across my neck, bends back my head so my neck is exposed, and goes to town with his lips.

With delicious excruciating movements, Keston Kips presses a line of steamy kisses down my throat.

Then, his mouth, hot from the sun, lowers onto my twin peaks as they push desperately through the crocheted holes of my top. He kisses one, then kisses the other.

His lips ease the flimsy material aside.

I gasp loudly when his teeth tug on a nipple, teasing it, pulling it into his mouth and suckling it like it's his and always has been.

"You like that, baby?" he asks, my nipple rolling across his tongue as he speaks.

Oh shit. This can't be real.

I nod my head.

My clitoris is weeping with desire for him to suck it too.

Neither of us says a word as he sucks and sucks, circling his tongue around and around my pointed nubs.

My knees feel like they'll sink onto the rock.

His arm holds up my body.

He lifts his head and looks into my eyes.

His are dark and hooded. A look of desire and longing in his stare.

I can feel him asking if he can touch me more.

I nod silently.

"Please," I whisper. "Please don't stop."

That's all he needs to hear. In one swoop, Keston raises up my entire body and slides his large, callused hand over my mound. He slips that same delicious finger into my hot channel and pumps it in and out, his mouth never leaving my nipples.

All the while, he presses his cupped palm against my pleasure center leaving my pussy feeling swollen and slick.

His mouth sucks on one nipple then the other. His big fingers stroke my clit gently. Then he presses his cupped palm hard against it as he slides his finger deeper inside my pussy.

My body bucks against his hand, pushing toward something it hasn't experienced in a long time. Pushing harder and harder.

"I want this," I groan softly. "I want this so badly."

"There's no one here to hear you," he says before sliding me down to the rock. He's standing in the shallow end of the pool. I'm lying with my back on the rock, legs spread open. I don't think this could possibly feel any better.

But then Keston Kips presses his thick, luscious lips right at my core. With one finger still stroking in and out of my slickness, his lips envelop my clit.

He presses, then releases my golden treasure so exquisitely that I feel my toes curling.

I could die right here with the intense ripples of pleasure coursing through me. My thighs drop open wider.

Keston's face is buried deep between them.

"You're as juicy as a ripe mango," he says, raising his head to check on me. My juices run down the sides of his mouth. He grins. "Fucking amazing, woman."

I arch my back for more. I'm hungry. Greedy. I want everything he's giving.

He seems to understand because he clamps his entire

mouth over my pussy, licking and sucking, swirling his tongue in and out. It's finger, tongue, finger, tongue. I lose track of what he's doing. I can't tell what's happening down there. All I know is I am close to exploding with pleasure.

My hips buck wildly under his other hand as he raises them, pressing my pussy right into his face, juices be damned.

It's then I feel the explosion coming. He feels it too. He slides a second finger into my pussy and ramps up the piston action.

His sucking never stops. He's rocking me with his fingers and sucking me with his mouth in an unending rhythm.

"Oh my God," I shout.

"Let it out," he mumbles, his face buried deep in my core. "Let it out, baby."

I grab his hair. I squeeze my thighs against his shoulders. "Oh my God," I cry. "Oh my God!"

And with one deep suck of everything holy, in and on me, I raise my hips to the sky and let out the loudest most primal scream I've ever heard. It goes on and on. It echoes to the far corners of our jungle paradise.

It reverberates through the trees. Birds fly off their branches.

And all the time I'm screaming, Keston Kips does not take his mouth off me. He knows I need this. I need it all.

Spasms ripple through my body. My entire being is unraveling. Keston holds me and never stops licking and sucking. He lashes my pussy until it's dry.

Afterwards, his palms find my tortured nipples and he cups them.

He drops his head on my stomach. My entire body rocks back and forth with him lying there. It's a complete release of my soul. The most intimate thing I've ever experienced.

I stroke his hair. He sighs. His dick is hard against my leg.

"Your turn?" I whisper.

He shakes his head. The stubble on his chin scratches my tender skin. "We have a lot of time. Don't worry about me. I'm good."

When my shaking subsides, he raises his head. A look of wonder lights up his face.

"You're glowing."

"You, too. That was amazing. I've never felt anything like that in my life." I see no reason to lie to him. Or pretend he didn't shake up my world.

He grins mischievously. "And we haven't even had sex yet."

# Chapter Thirty-Two

I'm naked in all my glory standing on a rock next to a man whose body is so beautiful he should be a statue in a museum. And I don't care how I compare.

I leap softly to another boulder and look at him over my shoulder. "You coming, buster?"

I have no idea where this minx act has come from, but I feel as if he's let something free inside of me.

Something I didn't even know was caged.

I am sultry. I'm a seducer. I'm a sex kitten.

Where is the serious, determined believer in habits and plans?

Keston's vibrant sexuality has awakened me. Even if we can never be a couple. He still makes me *want* to get my groove on big time. With him. Soon again.

"Well?"

His Adam's apple convulses.

"You ready to jump in?" I ask again.

He doesn't say anything about my breasts or the mound between my legs. But when I glance at him, his eyes are still darkly shadowed and full of something I haven't seen in a long, long time.

"Is that lust I see in your eyes?"

"Yes."

I thought I was making a joke. It fell flat.

I don't know what to say or do to a man who admits he's lusting after me. I'm forty and he's thirty-two. But he seems to know a lot more than I do in this situation.

"You're something else, woman," he says. "Now, let's go before I throw you down on this rock again and make you forget what's his name."

"Whose name?" I breathe, blood coursing through my veins.

"Exactly," he says.

I laugh. "You mean there's more to come."

"There's a lot more to come." He does not laugh.

The cool water is heavenly.

I sit on a rock as the water cascades around me.

The heavy drops thump against my shoulders and back like a masseuse's thumbs pressing me into oblivion.

I don't care about being naked. He's seen everything there is to see. My body feels womanly like Cleopatra lounging in a pool while her Marc Antony admires her.

The sun's rays stream across our pool. Actual beams of light pour down from the heavens.

I'm so relaxed, I don't realize I'm purring aloud. Like a cat. Or a lion, my purr is that full-throated.

Keston is diving under the water and popping up every few minutes, frolicking like a fish.

He swims over to my rock. Pulls himself up halfway out of the water. Bronzed triceps ripple. Drops of water roll slowly down his ripped abs, before hitting my leg.

"Having fun?" his dark eyes glimmer with the sun's rays.

I nod.

"I washed your swimsuit and beach dress."

I glance over to where he's spread our clothes on rocks to dry.

"Thank you," I say sweetly.

I don't know what's happened to me. If it's the refreshing river. The soothing sound of the waterfall. The sheer beauty of this place. Or the amazing loving I got. But I feel a sense of benevolence all around me.

I fling my arms into the sky. Drops fly from my fingertips

and rain down on Keston's curly hair. The sun makes the droplets shimmy and dance on his shoulders.

"You look like a mermaid," he says, tweaking my toes. "A sexy mermaid."

I lean my head back and let the sun-warmed waterfall cascade onto my face. Mostly to hide the blush creeping all over my skin.

"You can drink it," he says, shifting his body so it's closer to my own.

I snap my eyes open. "Really? Are you sure?"

He slides up on the wet rock, turning on his side to face me. He props his head up with one arm, biceps bulging like crazy.

"Yes, the moss on the rocks cleans the water. It's drinkable. Better even than *Perrier*," he says snidely.

Part of me has the nerve to feel wrongly accused.

I cup my hands to catch some water. I quickly raise it to my mouth to drink but a lot has seeped away between the cracks in my fingers.

I cup my hands and try again.

"Or you could just fill your empty Perrier bottle and pretend it's the expensive stuff."

He points to the side of the pool where he placed our two empty bottles of water.

I ignore him and tilt my head backward. A stream of water gushes down my throat. I swallow as much as I can before I shake my head, choking a bit.

"Ah!" he smiles, a twinkle in his eyes. "I see you've been training for this."

The way he says "this," I know he's not talking about swallowing water.

I swat his arm.

He tumbles into the river pool.

"Serves you right," I huff.

"Sensitive, huh?"

"Nope."

I suck my teeth the way I heard the islanders doing. It's rude sounding but seems to get the point across. "You think you can charm every woman. That's your problem."

He stands up waist-deep. Hands on hips.

"You mean I haven't charmed you yet?" He runs a hand through his hair. "Geez woman, what do I need to do?"

My face flames.

His breaks into a know-it-all smirk.

"You got something on your mind you wanna share with me?" He winks. "Or would you like a replay?" He eyes my breasts and pussy like a hunter on a mission. I cover my privates with my hands.

If my face was flaming before it's a volcano now.

I swat a handful of water his way. "You wish."

Why do I sound like a teenager flirting with the high school heartthrob?

"We don't have anything else to do for a couple of days," Keston says in a voice of reason. "We *could* have an epic time."

Now that we've found a source of fresh water to drink and bathe in, I'm not as worried about our time here. Tuesday will come. We'll be rescued. No one will need to know what happened here.

"So, you're saying, 'what happens in No Man's Land, stays in No Man's Land?'"

"You said it." He smiles sexily.

Why does this bartender's suggestion that we could keep having a delicious time, right here right now, and keep having it for days without a care in the world make my insides go wonky?

I narrow my eyes at him. "You seem pretty confident you can rock my world."

He stares back smugly. Like a stockbroker with an insider's tip. "I already did, sweetheart."

"Oh no," I groan. "You're back to being a dick."

As soon as I say the word, "dick," his eyes light up and he glances down at his perfect smooth thick member.

I look too. Big mistake. HUGE!

# Chapter Thirty-Three

When I was in college and in my early twenties, I was considered an "It girl." The one most likely to dance on a table and get busy with the captain of the football team.

But now . . . I'm more concerned about clients, getting

married, and making sure I don't end up like my mother—alone at sixty-three.

I'm only *forty!* I have plenty of time, right?

Except I don't. And being stuck on a deserted island with a Casanova bartender isn't helping me move forward. Sex with him would set me back. It would be like regressing to my twenties when it was just for fun. With no purpose in mind.

Fun, meaningless sex. As meaningless as this flower drifting down to the water, shimmering on the surface then disappearing underneath, soon to be forgotten.

I stare at the gossamer petals of the flower. I almost want to apologize to the poor plant for providing me with a moment of beauty before dying, while I complain it means nothing.

*Sheesh! Get out of your head, woman.*

*Great, now I sound like Keston.*

He's like a heat-seeking missile I'm trying to dodge. Or maybe *I'm* the heat-seeking missile and he's my target.

I don't dwell on it too much because I fall under the spell of the waterfall once more. But the images of having casual sex with Keston Kips play on a loop through my mind leaving me more confused than ever.

Later, with bottles filled with water, and dressed in clean, sun-dried swimsuits, Keston and I make our way back to the beach hut before the sun goes down.

"Are we lost?" I ask as we meander over rocks and roots.

"We can't get lost."

"Speak for yourself."

He points in the direction of trees that look like every other direction to me.

"You just need to listen for the surf breaking on shore." He cups his ear toward the direction he'd pointed.

I shift the giant bowling ball of a breadfruit I'm carrying from one hand to the other. It's another of Keston's forest gifts. We won't discuss his first one. Ha!

"I don't have your bionic hearing. I can't tell the difference between surf breaking and tree branches waving in the air if you must know."

"Train your ears to understand the sounds of things."

I roll my eyes at the idea that I'd be here long enough to need to know the difference.

"I'll just depend on you." I say it jokingly. But it's no joke. I'd definitely get lost without Keston Kips by my side leading the way.

I'm not sure how that makes me feel. To be so dependent on a man.

Not to mention I'm punch drunk on the soothing sound of the waterfall. That's the only thing I'm hearing in my mind.

Gazing upwards at the towering trees, birds flitting about in the cooling air, I can't imagine New York City or my condo at all. It feels as if years of stress from making work and life decisions have drained right out of me. And not because of that mind-blowing orgasm I had.

It's because there aren't any options to choose from.

It's funny how easy it is to simplify when you don't have choices.

Now, as we tread over fallen leaves and tree roots, careful to avoid the many spider webs glittering like lace amongst the tree branches, I ask about the large breadfruits he foraged for us in the woods.

He explains how he'll roast them on the fire. "They're delicious any way you cook them.

Every family on the island has a breadfruit tree in their yard," he says. "You can never go hungry when you have breadfruit."

"Why? I ask.

He swings the breadfruit he's carrying by its sturdy stalk. "Breadfruits flower and grow all year long. So they're always available. And they're nutritious."

I love the way he explains things to me. He never makes me feel silly or ignorant. And his protectiveness is obvious.

At one point at the falls, I had felt sleepy. But with only rocks and tree roots, there was no place for me to lay down.

"Just put your head here, woman," Keston had insisted, lying flat on a rock and patting his chest.

"Right, that looks comfy." I spluttered rudely. "Your chest is as hard as these rocks."

He had the nerve to beam. "Thank you."

"I'd give anything for a fat dude right now. One with lots of cushion."

I was rewarded with a deep belly laugh.

I laughed with him.

A memory flashed through me. After a few months of dating Marcus, we were lying in bed, him on his laptop, me reading a romance novel.

He'd frowned at my choice of reading material, saying it had little to no value and I should read something more enriching.

I'd burst out laughing. I mean seriously, he had to be joking.

I recall expecting him to laugh with me. But he didn't. He wasn't joking.

Instead, he shook his head, an irritable look marring his perfect eyebrows. "I want more for you. Sorry."

Was he sorry I didn't want more for myself? I couldn't tell. But the next day I received a package at work.

It was a stack of books about leadership, goal fulfillment, and time management. I was stunned. That stack of books made me feel as small as an ant.

I never let Marcus see me reading a romance novel again. I kept them to myself. It wasn't the only thing I kept to myself throughout our five-year relationship.

Now, after Keston's explanation about breadfruits, a thought filters through my mind. Maybe I'll read my romance book *to* Keston. We have lots of time. He looks like he'd be open to it. Especially the steamy parts. I only hope he doesn't get the wrong idea.

*Or the right one*, a voice whispers in my head.

Back at our camp, as I refer to our tiki hut and fire circle, I take up my walking stick and press the edge into the palm tree trunk.

Keston glimpses me and asks, "Are you carving our initials? CJ and KK?"

I roll my eyes. This guy is such an optimist.

I step back and point at the two tiny marks I've scratched into the trunk. "I didn't want to hurt Prince Harry," I say, patting the tree like it's my friend.

He nods. "What's that though?"

"I'm marking our days on the island. Keeping a calendar."

"How long are you planning to be here, woman?"

I shrug. "It's what people do. When they're stuck somewhere."

His eyes darken. "This is really horrible for you, isn't it?"

"Isn't it for you?"

He shakes his head. "Nope. I kind of like it."

I shiver as if he said he eats frogs.

"I don't think I'm cut out for surviving on a deserted island. I can't wait to take a hot shower. Or eat a delicious steak. Or . . ."

Keston puts up a hand. "Let's not play the 'I can't wait' game. Let's focus on the here and now. Which means we need to cook this breadfruit and maybe catch some fish for dinner tonight. Those bananas we munched on at the waterfall aren't enough."

"Okay. But I still can't wait for . . ."

"Watch out!" he shouts.

"What!" I scream and spin around wildly.

Keston grabs my walking stick and thunders after something in the bushes.

I hunch my shoulders and try to make myself as small as possible. Fear settles like ice water in my stomach.

I can't hear Keston anymore.

The only sounds are the rustle of palm fronds and the drumming of waves on the sand. I sit and wait.

And wait.

And wait.

Half an hour must have passed already from the way the sun is sinking fast into the ocean.

While the sun slides its bright orange orb into the sea, mosquitoes swarm around my head, buzzing like a chorus of bees. I glance with trepidation at the darkening woods where Keston disappeared. Soon the bats will fly out of there. And then what?

I swing my fists at the mosquitos helplessly. My beach bag

hangs from a tree branch all the way across the sand. I'm too frightened to get up and retrieve my bug repellant from it.

I close my eyes and pray, "Please come back. Please come back."

A scary thought arises. He may be annoying and full of himself, but Keston Kips makes me feel safe. What if he doesn't come back?

Should I go look for him? I glance towards the dark woods. What was he chasing? Where did he go? And what about the bats?!

I press my eyelids down tightly and pray aloud in a shaky voice. "Please come back. Please come back."

I can barely speak over the lump of fear forming in my throat.

I kneel in the sand until my knees ache. I must get up. I can't stay in this spot all night.

Slowly, as if my legs are full of lead, I stand up and scuttle over to Keston's black dry bag.

I'll light a fire. It'll keep the bats away at least.

I search inside his small hip bag and find the lighter. "Thank you," I whisper.

Okay, what did Keston do to start the fire? I force my mind to think back to yesterday evening. He was tearing apart the dried-out coconuts. Making a pile of coconut husks.

Luckily there's plenty more of those strewn around Prince Harry.

"Thanks, Your Royal Highness," I whisper.

I stack the pile of coconut husks one on top of the other and lean forward to light the pile from underneath.

I cup the tiny flame emerging from the purple lighter. The breeze is much stronger than last night. Almost as if rain is coming, which I hope and pray it isn't.

"Ouch!" I cry. The flame scorches my fingers.

I try again, pushing the lighter towards the husks and leaning forward to blow on it.

"Hurry up," I whisper. The bats have returned. They're winging circles and swooping closer and closer to me. I can see their shadowy forms in the dusk.

My heartbeat triples in speed. My breath comes in shallow bursts. "Hurry," I beg the lighter. "Hurry and light." I'm doing my best not to scream and run and hide.

My hand holding the lighter is shaking so much, I reach with my other hand to hold it steady.

With both arms outstretched, I shut my eyes and shove the lighter into the pile of dried husks. I don't care if I get burned. I'm not moving my hand until the fire starts.

I hear rustling sounds in the blackness surrounding me. Night comes so fast in the Caribbean. And with it, the strangest sounds.

Unlike last night with the moon and bright stars, tonight there is a blank canvas covering the sky. I can't see a thing.

"Oh God, help me."

I feel a flare at my fingertips. It burns my fingers. A piece of dried husk catches on fire. I cradle the small flickering flame.

What did I see Keston doing?

"How did he get it to crackle and pop?" I ask the sky.

"You gotta give it oxygen. Blow on it."

I leap up. I can barely see his face from the light of the small fire. But it's Keston. I race toward him. Throw my arms around his neck.

Before he can wrap his arms around me, I step back and poke him in the chest. Hard.

"Ouch, woman."

"Where did you go? Don't ever leave me again. I can't believe you left me here with the bats."

The fear I was feeling unleashes into tears. Hot, angry, scared tears.

I hiccup. "Never again. Promise."

"Oh, CJ. I'm sorry. I didn't know it would take me so long. Come here." He reaches out hard muscled arms and pulls me to his chest.

"I promise."

He leans back and I lean back, and we stare into each other's eyes. I can feel his heart beating under my hand pressed to his chest. It feels solid and strong. Like he can handle anything.

Suddenly, there's a loud snapping sound and flames leap into the sky.

"Wow, you made a crazy fire. And built a perfect fire circle. Check you out."

I turn to stare at the flames leaping into the air.

"It's a *fucking* miracle," I say.

Our joint laughter frees something inside me.

A feeling of optimism rises within. Keston's kind of optimism, which I thought was just for fools and children.

"It's you and me, CJ. We got this." Keston kisses the top of my head.

It's the kind of kiss you can expect from a father or brother.

Nothing to write home about.

Except this little kiss leaves me giddy with pleasure.

I can't stop smiling under the cover of darkness.

And I can't help thinking, I wonder what this adventure will bring next.

# Chapter Thirty-Four

"You want me to eat that thing? It's out of the question. I prefer to starve."

Keston Kips is swinging the carcass of a large green-brown iguana like it's a prize. The lizard or reptile or whatever it is looks as wide as my thigh. Its long tail is spiky and dragging on the sand.

"You killed it?" I ask, feeling sorry for the iguana now that it's dead.

"Yes," he says proudly. "It was an epic battle. But I won. I saw him on the branch right next to your head. They camouflage themselves very well. You would have lost it if you came face to face with him."

I think he wants me to congratulate him. Man killed a beast and all that, but I'm still feeling sorry for the iguana.

"I've never eaten anything other than seafood, beef, and chicken. I don't even eat pork. I can't eat that . . ." I shiver. "*Beast.*"

Shaking his head, Keston drops the iguana on the sand close to the fire. "I have to clean it first. You might want to look away. But once it's cooked, you'll love it. It tastes like chicken."

"I'll pass. How are you going to cut it open anyway? *Ugh.*"

He laughs. I never imagined I'd be so happy to hear his laugh.

He pulls out a knife from his dry bag. It's a small knife for what looks to be a big job.

"Stand back."

He doesn't have to tell me twice. I grab my beach bag from Prince Harry and scurry to the far side of the fire where I can't witness the massacre.

"You want to hear a story?" I ask.

"Sure," he grunts. I hear a lot of straining and tugging and try to block out the sounds by raising my voice. I crack open my romance novel and turn to the beginning.

"Chapter 1," I start. The fire's shadowy flames dance across the pages. My voice rises and falls with the shadows.

For the next hour, I read aloud to Keston as he prepares dinner the old-fashioned way. By killing and cleaning it first.

I read about the couple's meet cute. Their sexy banter. Their slow burn.

I'm transported right off the island into a world of forbidden love, betrayal, passion, and more.

"I feel as if I'm seeing a movie," Keston remarks when I stop to take a sip of water.

I nod, water filling up my dry throat. "Yes. Her writing is sooooo good."

"And your reading makes it better."

I think I blush. Maybe it's the fire making my skin warmer.

After Keston has wrestled the iguana into a cooking position on open coals, I collect more coconut husks and throw them onto my miracle blaze. I try not to think about the reptile roasting on our jerry-rigged bonfire. But the fire crackles and pops as the meat begins cooking.

I continue reading the story. The female main character harbors a secret desire. Not surprisingly, it clashes with the main male character's own secret desire.

"Why do people fall for a forbidden romance?" I ask, stopping for another sip of the cool water we bottled from the waterfall.

Keston stops stoking the fire. His face is streaked with perspiration and soot. He looks hot. And not just in the too close to the fire hot.

"Maybe they're bored?" he suggests.

I shake my head no. "Too simple. Must be a desire to have what you shouldn't."

A loud laugh escapes his lips.

"What?" I ask, vexed.

"Nothing."

"No, it's something. People don't laugh for no reason."

"It's the way you analyze love."

"What's wrong with the way I analyze it?"

He stands up. The firelight plays havoc on his bare chest.

He looks like he could be or should be on the cover of this book.

I shake my head. "Well?"

"Love can't be analyzed. It just is."

"Oh really?"

"Yes, really. Love doesn't have any logic. It's random. And unexpected. And . . . ," he grins. "Spectacular."

"You're thinking of sex. Not love."

"I'm thinking of it all."

I scoff. Dig my toes into the cool sand. "Right."

"You really believe people have no control over who they fall in love with? Like it doesn't stem from the way they were raised? Or the things they long for? Or . . . ," I stop.

"Or what?"

My voice drops. "Circumstances. Like being in the same place at the same time."

He hoots a laugh. "Absolutely not."

"How are you so sure?"

"Because we're here. Stuck on a deserted island together. No one else around. And according to you, *we're* not falling in love."

"Exactly!" I pounce on his answer. "We're not."

"Glad we cleared that up." But his voice doesn't sound smug or glad or anything like that.

"Me too," I mutter. A weird sinking feeling comes over me. As if I wish we hadn't cleared it up after all. But that can't be right.

He's a bartender living on a remote island in the Caribbean.

I'm a partner in a top-tier law firm in New York City. I have a mortgage and access to some of the best restaurants in the world. He has . . . hmmm . . . I don't know what he has. Or what he dreams of having. Or anything about him.

Other than he can make amazing drinks. He can fish, hunt, and cook his own food. Oh, and he can make me see fireworks.

Can't forget that.

I return to the pages of my romance novel.

Maybe it's better to read about a make-believe romance than to fantasize about one of my own.

# Chapter Thirty-Five

Dinner is the roasted breadfruit with sea water sprinkled across the buttery yellow starchy insides which look like potato but taste chewy like bread. I suppose that's where it gets its name.

"This is my first time eating breadfruit." I scoop up the

roasted pieces with a "spoon" Keston made from a sharp piece of coconut shell.

"Yummy." I lean back against Prince Harry, my legs straight in front of me. The sand is cool at night. The mosquitoes have disappeared. The bats are nowhere to be seen.

Probably on a bat mission. Keaston explained how important the fruit bats are to the ecosystem. Knowing they eat insects and pests that damage crops as well as pollinate fruit trees, I respect the creatures now.

I still don't want them near me.

Which is more than I can say for our bartender. I *need* him near me.

I peek at him cutting his precious iguana steak into bite-sized pieces. I shrink when he offers me a piece.

I clutch my throat. "Absolutely not."

"It's a prized dish on St. Nicholas. You should try it. It's part of our *culture*."

I bite my lip as if I'm afraid he'll force me to eat it. "I'm happy with this breadfruit. Also, part of your culture. Maybe tomorrow we can catch more fish."

"Making plans already?"

"What's wrong with thinking ahead?"

"Nothing. What's wrong with thinking of right now?"

We finish eating in silence. I don't share that I'm planning on looking for breadfruit at the West Indian supermarkets in New York. That is far ahead indeed.

After dinner, we toss our leaf plates into the fire and wash our hands at the edge of the sea.

"The aloe should be finished draining." Keston points to the aloe leaves he foraged from the forest while we were at the waterfall.

He examines the aloe leaves which he turned upside down

pointy part skyward to drain it of the yellow toxins that he said would stain our clothes.

Staining my clothes is the least of my worries. I'm excited to feel the aloe on my parched skin.

Keston cuts the aloe into thick slices. Sticky gel seeps out from both sides. "Hold it like this," he says, demonstrating how to grab a piece of aloe and rub it on my skin.

"Or would you like me to do it for you?"

I cough. Do I want to feel his hands on my body again? Or show him how self-sufficient I can be?

"Be in the moment, remember?" He waves the aloe that is oozing its gel onto his hands.

I stick out an arm. "Okay, you do it."

So much for self-sufficiency.

Keston drags one of our sleeping mats next to the fire while holding the aloe plant high. He pats the mat and straightens up.

I get the idea and sit down.

Keston kneels in the sand and rubs my calves with the gel. My skin soaks up the moisture like a baby lamb drinking milk.

"Take off your dress."

"I'm not wearing my swimsuit underneath."

He sighs. "I know. I need to rub your back and shoulders."

I do as he asks. I stick my ass up in the air to wiggle out of the long dress. He has a full view of every nook I possess.

Any nervousness I had earlier about my naked body is gone. In its place is a little pride. And something else. Something like acceptance.

It is what it is. I eat healthy. I exercise. I should be proud of my God-given attributes. Firm legs, still perky breasts, and a pussy that apparently won't stop filling with juices whenever this man is near.

I can't see his face, but I hear the smokiness in his voice when he says, "Very nice."

He rubs the gel into my back and buttocks like he's kneading dough.

"Flip over."

I do as he asks. I lie on my back. Naked and exposed.

He rubs aloe together in his hands. "You're beautiful, CJ."

"Thanks?"

"It's not a question. It's the truth. Your skin is soft and smooth like honey. I could lick you all over. All day and night."

I shiver. Close my eyes. Is he giving me lines? But why would he? We've already been intimate. I mean we haven't had actual sex as he says. Is this his version of foreplay?

"Be in the moment," he whispers, as his hands glide the soothing gel up the insides of my thighs. One leg, then the other. "Relax, you deserve this. I'm impressed with how well you've adapted to beach life. You are strong. You are capable. You are fine as hell."

His voice, his lips, and the way he caresses my skin are all part of a song, each a note or chorus, a bar or riff, coming together in perfect harmony.

I find myself being lulled into a peaceful sleep. I'm floating on air. Far away into the night sky.

But then, a rock-hard penis hits my leg as he leans over me.

"Sorry," he says, pushing it out of the way. But how can he move the mountain of swollen flesh protruding from his slim hips.

"You have a beautiful penis," I breathe out. "In case you didn't know it."

My every nerve end is tingling. Sparking like a million fireflies. He's got a cock that won't quit. And I have a pussy that begs for it.

He sits back on his haunches. "I wasn't massaging you for sex."

"Sure, you weren't."

At the strained look on his face, my teasing voice fizzles. "What's wrong?"

"There's something about you."

I prop up on my elbows. "The fact that I told you I was sex-starved on the first night we met? Maybe that's it?"

He rubs his hands full of aloe gel down my chest making sure to get under my arms and around my nipples. I swear if he goes any closer to them, I'll flip him over and have my way with his pulsating prick.

"Not that."

"Then what?"

He looks up at the night sky. The fire has died down so we can see it without the light pollution. Stars glitter and glow where earlier they hid from me. A long streaky galaxy pours its light upon us.

"You know what I thought when I first met you?"

"No." It's my voice that's husky and low now.

He shifts away from me. Knees in the sand wiping the last remnants of the aloe gel on his legs. "I thought you were Lucy fallen from the sky. You were wearing a dress that sparkled. Kind of like the beach cover-up, but under the moonlight it really shone."

Whoa! I did not expect him to get poetic.

"Are you talking about the star that is a giant diamond in the sky? The one you told me about on the boat ride?"

His head bends down. "Corny huh?"

"No." I sit up fully. My breasts glisten under the sheen of the aloe gel. "It's sweet. Why did you think I was a star?"

"Because I've never run into anyone on that hillside at night. It's where I go to look at the stars. It's kind of my spot. I have an old telescope a guest gave me ten years ago. I can see the moon and Saturn and Jupiter. Never Lucy, though. But then there you were, all sparkly and shiny, and so pretty. I thought, *there's my Lucy.*"

I grip his hand. "That's lovely. I've always wanted to name my daughter Lucy. If I have one," I add quickly."

"Funny," he tilts his head, gazing deeply into my eyes. "Me too."

My massage is forgotten. Or pushed aside for the moment.

"I believe you weren't trying to have sex with me. I'm sorry I mistook your intentions."

His eyes flare. "Oh, don't get me wrong. I want to fuck you so bad. I only have one condom in my bag. Unless you have some, I don't want to waste our chance."

My eyes open wide. "Just when I was thinking you're sweet and nice."

He gives a lopsided grin. "Sorry."

"I knew it was too good to be true. But I liked your Lucy story."

"I like everything about you."

"So far," I murmur. "There's stuff you don't know."

"Everyone has secrets. It doesn't make you less special."

"I'm not sure about that."

At that moment, the sky dims down its light. A cloud hovers blocking the stars and moon. Like God pulled a curtain on our slumber party.

"The breeze feels different tonight. And the clouds are darker than I've seen in a long time," Keston observes.

"It feels as if we're the last two humans on earth." I squeeze his hand.

"It feels as if we're getting a storm." He walks to the edge of the sea.

I wrap my arms around my shoulders, suddenly remembering I'm naked. A regular occurrence now.

Keston is eyeing the sky with intensity.

I appreciate the darkness. It's the perfect cover for protecting my deepest secret. One I've not told anyone in the world.

Since being on this island, castaway from civilization, the secret has been playing on my mind. As if it has been waiting years for me to lose all the distractions of the regular world to emerge into the light.

# Chapter Thirty-Six

Day three on the island is a Sunday. A day I usually lay in bed reading a book, before hustling to complete all the chores I've procrastinated doing during the week.

I order food online to be delivered. I throw in a load of laundry. I pay bills. I answer pesky emails.

And I talk for an hour on the phone with my mother. I turn

on a timer. I can't be dragged into a too-long conversation about her neighbors or the church or whom she despises now.

Every week she asks me the same question. When am I coming to spend time with her upstate in our small hometown that I left behind to attend college at Howard University in Washington D.C.

Ever since my parents' separation when I was ten years old, then their divorce when I was twelve, mom refuses to take an interest in anything but me.

She doesn't date. She doesn't hang out with her girlfriends because they're still married to their spouses, and she feels left out. She doesn't have hobbies that I know of.

My weekly Sunday conversation is not my only connection to my mother. But it is the most consistent one. Ever since what happened when I was a junior in college.

This Sunday, none of those chores await me. Mom knows I'm on vacation so she's not expecting our weekly call. My girlfriends will think I'm following their orders and having a great time focusing on myself and getting some action. If they only knew.

So, technically, I can lay on my newly braided sleeping mat all day long and do nothing but read.

If it weren't so *boiling* hot.

Damn, sweat is running rivers down my chest.

I look outside the tiki hut for Keston. As usual, he's not there. Probably off on some Johnny Depp pursuit, like looking for limes to make drinks with the coconuts he cut open last night.

I head to my "bathroom," and splash about in the sea, washing off sand, dunking my hair, and tying it back with my headband.

One look at my dress and I want to cry. It's crumpled, the crocheted threads are unraveling, and it looks like I'm wearing a dead bird. Versace is not the designer of choice for deserted islands.

Calvin Klein's practical minimalist wear would work. Or better yet, some sturdy sweatpants and tank tops from Walmart.

As I stand at the edge of the shore, shading my eyes and staring at the horizon for any passing boats, a shadowy form appears in the water near my feet.

I squeal and jump back. The shape dives and pops back up a few feet away.

"Oh, it's you, my beautiful tortoise friend."

I don't know if it's the same one, but it has the same diamond yellow colorings, the same size, and it's looking at me like it knows me.

"How are you today? Only two more days and I'm outta here."

The turtle's shell is as round as a giant frisbee. Its webbed feet poke out on all sides and paddle back and forth in the shallow water.

Do people visiting the island feed this turtle? Maybe it's used to people talking to it.

I stoop and it dives. It doesn't go far. It pops up a few feet away.

I decide to name the turtle. "How about 'Sandy.' Like in Grease. You look like a Sandy. And you live on a beach."

The turtle pats the water with her large flippers. She approves. Yeah!

I admire Sandy's aquatic tricks until she disappears.

Then I stroll along the shore, picking up shells, tossing rocks into the sea, and watching my footprints disappear beneath the incoming waves.

The waves are bigger than before. They hit the sand with more force than during the last two days. The sky is greyish brown. A color I've never seen in the sky before.

Above the sound of the waves, I hear my name being called.

"*CJ!*"

"What?" I shout back into the air.

"Here!"

I gaze around. "Where?"

"Up!"

I glance at the sky. I cast my eyes on the tree trunks. Nothing.

"Up here!"

I focus on what Keston taught me yesterday by the waterfalls. If I want to spot birds or wildlife, I must look for the unusual pattern in the scene. Unusual color, unusual movements. I apply that test and search the scenery.

I see his dark brown muscular legs first. They're clinging to a tree like a sloth. Or a lemur.

One arm is wrapped around the top of the trunk. With his other hand, he shades his eyes as he peers out at the horizon. My heart flutters. He's hotter than any pirate in the movies.

"Do you see a boat?" I jump up and down.

"No."

"Oh." I stop jumping. "Then what is it?"

He points straight ahead.

I look but I can't see anything unusual. I focus on the bigger picture and search for clues. Discrepancies in the patterns of sea and sky.

"Just tell me," I holler. "I don't see anything."

As soon as those words leave my mouth, I notice it. Or rather, *them*. And they're heading our way. Like witches on broomsticks.

I don't know what to call the dark swirling furies out on the sea.

"Are those tornados?" I shout over the whooshing of the breeze.

"Water tornados." He leaps down.

Fear creeps up my spine. "Are we in danger?"

"They can be deadly. They mean severe thunderstorms are coming or even a hurricane is forming or has already formed over the sea."

"But it's March. Your hurricane season doesn't start until June."

"Tell that to climate change."

I wring my hands. "What does this mean?"

He bites his bottom lip. One arm slips around my shoulders in a protective hug. "It means we need to head inland. Away from the sea. If a hurricane is coming," he points at the grey clouds swirling above us, "then our safest place is higher up. On a mountain or hill."

"But what about the boat that's coming to get us on Tuesday. We can't leave the beach. We'll miss them."

He turns dark eyes on me. His bottom lip catches between his teeth. "I'm afraid they won't come if there's bad weather. Not with a possible hurricane or severe thunderstorms on the horizon."

Panic grips my heart. Bile stings my throat. "They must come. It's been two whole days. I can't stay here much longer."

All the ways I've been holding on come to a boil like a pot of milk bubbling over.

"I can't be stuck here forever."

Keston looks as forlorn as I do.

"Nobody's coming to rescue us, are they?" I wail.

# Chapter Thirty-Seven

I cry for a good half hour.

Then I get up, my mind focused on one thing. Hurricane or no hurricane, I am getting us off this island. I am done with Keston's "make the best of it" attitude. I need plans. I need action. I need to rescue us myself.

I walk away from Keston. He's doing something with a stick and a coconut.

I don't ask.

But the stick gives me an idea. I grab my trusty walking stick and traipse up and down the beach until I find what I'm looking for.

A wide clearing where the waves don't reach. With my tattered dress blowing behind me, I draw the letters H E L P as large as I can in the clearing. Far enough from the sea but still visible from the sky.

I race around gathering bright red hibiscus from flowering trees a few feet into the forest. I consider pink oleanders, but Keston said oleanders are poisonous, so I leave them alone.

I prick my fingers on the thorny fuchsia bougainvillea, but I gather them into my arms.

With a pile of flowers next to me, I kneel in the sand and carefully outline the letters HELP with the multicolored blooms.

If it wasn't an emergency, it could be a beach wedding decoration. Except it would say, *Just Married*.

I want a Just Married sign in my life. After I get off this island I'm going to find my perfect match. My one true love. No more time to waste.

I tuck the last flower into the crease of the P and stand up brushing off my hands and knees.

Anyone flying overhead can see this sign. Although I haven't seen any planes in the past two days. But hurricane hunters, those mavericks who fly into tropical storms to gather information, might see my sign. They could come to our rescue.

It's better than waiting for a boat that may never come.

Keston sits on a tree stump whittling his stick with the sharp edge of a coconut shell.

"Why don't you get up and help me?" I snarl. "I want to make a bonfire at the edge of the sea. We can light it with your rum. Even if no one on St. Nick sees it, someone flying overhead might."

He says calmly, "I'm doing something else."

"What?" I huff. "My knees hurt from kneeling in the sand. My back aches from sleeping on the ground. I'm sweaty and I've had grains of sand in my mouth for days now. What can you possibly be doing with that stick that is more important?"

"Making a spear."

"Why do we need a spear?" Anxiety ramps up in my belly.

He twirls it like it's a baton. Examines the pointed edge. Resumes scraping it with the coconut shell and a large stone.

"I saw some fish in the rock pools over there." He points the stick toward the rocky end of the long beach where I had entered the sea the day I almost drowned. I don't go over there. Bad memories and all.

"Oh."

"I'm going to catch some fish. Dry them in the sun to take with us when we go looking for higher ground."

"So, I'm planning for us to be rescued before the storm arrives and you're planning for us to still be here? Make that make sense. Please!"

I can hear the hostility and irritability in my tone. I don't like how I sound. I wrote a term paper on *Lord of the Flies* in high school. I know how this scenario can go if one of us gets crazed with power. Or delusional with contempt for the other.

I eye his spear. He's the only one of us with a weapon.

Wait! What am I thinking? He's not going to hurt me.

"Are you okay?"

With hands on my hips, I say, "There's nothing to be okay about. So don't ask me that."

If this were me and Marcus, I'd never speak to him like this. I'd bite my tongue until it bled. I'd bury my anger. I'd do . . . *anything* not to show him this edgy side of me. This complaining, snarly, hot-tempered self.

Keston's face breaks into a wicked smile. "I like this side of you."

"If you say I'm cute when I'm mad, I'll stab you with your own spear."

He gurgles with laughter.

"What are you laughing about?"

*"Ahahahahaha!"* His laughter escalates.

Oh my God, is he going crazy?

He bends forward. Mouth wide open. Eyes crinkled in the corners. He swipes the bandana off his curls and wipes tears of glee from his eyes.

"You're scaring me."

He laughs so hard he falls off his tree stump.

A weird sound crawls up my throat. Watching Keston practically kill himself with laughter I can't help it. I laugh too.

We're two lunatics staggering around the beach holding our sides, tears streaming down our faces.

Until we collapse on the sand. We flop backward. The clouds loom heavy above.

I swish my arms and legs back and forth carving a sand angel.

He scoots out of my way.
"You know what, woman?"
"What?"
"I'm glad it's you I'm stuck here with."

# Chapter Thirty-Eight

The shared laughter doesn't make the impending storm less frightful. That whole, laughter is the best medicine advice, is a distraction from real problems.

After the fun and games are over, it's back to business. Or, in our case, it's back to figuring out a rescue plan *before* the storm hits.

Spearfishing and stockpiling fish is the emergency measure in case we don't succeed.

"Okay, boss what do you need me to do?"

I direct Keston to pile coconut palms high at the edge of the clearing next to my HELP sign.

He points to a spot further away and says we can't have smoke blowing over the sign.

"Right," I say, glad he's on board.

Back and forth we trudge through the sand dragging long palm branches behind us. The branches are browned from the sun and salt water and have been lying about for ages. They're now serving a good purpose.

"Let's not tear off any new branches," I say. "Especially from my tree."

He snorts. "I'll make sure not to touch precious Prince Harry's leaves."

Walking up and down the sloping sand in flip flops slows me down. I kick them off so I can work faster.

Neither of us speaks as the sun burns through the strange whitish-grey-colored sky. When my feet blister on the hot seashore, I don't say a word.

When the sun scorches my scalp, I curse under my breath and haul the branches one by one. When sweat runs down my face and into my eyes so I can barely see, I squeeze my eyes closed and walk blindly.

No Man's Land has become a hellish paradise.

"Next?" Keston stands next to the pile of leaves. It's as high as his shoulders.

I squint against the haze shimmering in the atmosphere.

Our pile of palm leaves is as high as the one in the *Pirates of the Caribbean* sequel when Johnny Depp and Keira Knightley were stuck on that island. The fact that I'm creating rescue plans from a Johnny Depp movie proves my level of desperation.

"Coconut husks. We should put a bunch of dried coconut husks under the leaves to really get it smoking," I say, swaying in the heat.

"Okay, but how about we stop and take a quick swim and

catch some fish? That way we can cook the fish while firing up this heap."

I suck on my lips. They're blistering in the hot sun. As are my shoulders. I'm running out of sunblock, so I've used it sparingly.

Keston marches toward the tiki hut. "Let's drink some water. You don't look too great."

"Thanks. I'm trying to save us."

"No seriously. You look like you're ready to pass out."

"I don't have *time* to pass out." My knees buckle. The sand tilts toward me fast. Before I hit the ground, strong arms scoop under my legs and across my shoulders.

"You were saying?"

Keston carries me easily like he does this all the time.

Up the sandy slope. Across to our tiki hut. He sets me gently on a sleeping mat. Before my flaming head hits the mat, I groan, "I'm sorry."

Keston raises my head and tilts the Perrier bottle of spring water into my mouth.

"Drink as much as you need. I can fill them up again."

I sip slowly. My throat has become so parched it hurts to swallow.

Keston cradles my head in his lap. He tilts the bottle to my mouth again.

"We're not working in the hot sun anymore. There's a reason we islanders take naps in the middle of the day. Somewhere cool and air-conditioned. Or in a hammock in the shade where it's breezy."

"That sounds nice."

"It is. I have a double hammock in case you're interested. You'd fit next to me real good."

I scoff. "Keep wishing."

He tilts the bottle. "Drink up. You're not better yet. You haven't cried or complained in hours."

I raise my hand to smack his arm, but I lack the strength. My hand falls back to my side.

"Just wait until I recover from . . . whatever this is."

"Heat stroke. People die from it." His jokey voice belies the concern in his eyes.

"I thought that was only in the desert."

"Nope. It can happen anywhere you're exposed to the sun and your body temperature rises."

"I'm a real hot chick, huh?" My eyelids feel heavy. I can't laugh at my pathetic joke.

He shakes my shoulders. "Drink more water. And yeah. You've been a hot chick since Day 1."

"I want to sleep," I breathe.

His legs jiggle under my body. He raises my head and presses cool lips on my forehead.

Is he seriously trying to kiss me now? I look terrible.

"What . . . are you . . . doing?" I stutter.

"I'm testing your body temperature."

I can't respond. My entire body is on fire.

# Chapter Thirty-Nine

Forget about lighting the bonfire. Forget about spearfishing for the storm. Keston Kips kisses my forehead and gasps.

"CJ. You're burning up." His voice shakes.

He smooths back my hair. "We gotta get your body temperature down."

I'm watching all of this from a position floating over my body. I've disconnected from my flesh and blood. I'm a soul floating in an out-of-body limbo.

Keston gathers me close to his chest. He leaves the shelter of the tiki hut and stands on the hot beach surveying the sea. Big-fisted waves smack the shoreline, hitting like a boxer decimating his opponent.

Keston spins around and lurches into the forest. He carries me as easily as if I were a rag doll. My arms are drooping down, my head lolling backward. I look worse than a rag doll.

Wake up, I shout at myself. This is not the time to fall asleep.

Keston kisses my lips. I feel it as light as butterfly wings. Almost as if it didn't happen.

"You got this, CJ. Don't stop pestering me now."

Pestering *him*. Damn, he's gonna get it later.

Keston Kips runs in his bare feet. He clasps me close to his body as he dodges low-hanging branches, leaps over rocks, and skims leaf piles left and right.

In my semi-unconscious state, I hear the water rushing over the rocks. I concentrate on Keston's face so I don't lose consciousness completely.

His eyes are wide. His lips are pressed together in a grimace. His focus is intense.

As soon as he gets near the waterfall, he whooshes out a breath. "You're going to be alright, baby."

I can't answer him. I squeeze his finger to let him know I hear him. He looks shocked at my touch.

He recovers and gives a Usain Bolt sprint right into the cool clear pool of water holding me in his arms. It's like a baptism. He dips down and we both go under. Then he sputters upward and takes me with him.

The idiot does it again. He dips us both down under the surface. Then springs back up. He does it a third time.

This time I come up coughing water.

"Dude," I choke. "Are you trying to drown me?"

"No, yes, maybe."

His laughter rings out across the rock walls. He sounds happy and delirious at the same time.

I relax in his arms. "What happened?"

He cups water in one hand and pours it over my head. I shake the drops from my ears and nose. "You're doing it again."

"Sorry. I need to cool you down some more. Just chill please."

"Chill?"

He shrugs, kisses my lips, splashes more water on my forehead.

"When did we start kissing on the lips?"

His eyes spark. "Just now. When I thought you were dying."

"And you're who? Prince Charming? Kissing the princess alive?"

He shrugs. "Yeah, someone's gotta do it."

I smile up at him. "Well, I'm glad it's you."

Keston refuses to let me stand, walk, or do anything but lay on his lap in the pool's shallow end. He's worried my body temperature will rise again.

I'm worried too. Being disconnected from my body was weird, floating like a genie in the air.

"How long do we need to stay here?" I ask. "Shouldn't we be fishing for tomorrow?"

He shakes his curly hair. Water droplets drizzle on me. I don't complain.

This view from my position against his pecs is superb. Strong, square jaw covered in two days of stubble. Strapping shoulders that would make even Hercules jealous. And tight dark nipples that adorn his pecs to perfection.

He has the bone structure and deep lines a fashion designer and sculptor would fight over.

"Why are you staring at me like that?"

I gulp. "Like what?"

"Like you want to spray whipped cream on me and have me for dessert."

If he only knew.

"Can we go to the beach and prepare for the storm? And light the bonfire."

"No rush," he says. "You *need* to stay in the shade and the cool water until the sun goes down."

I glance at the sky. "That's hours away. What are we going to do until then?"

His eyes spark even more. "I could think of a thing or two."

I shiver in delight. "I'd love it. Are you going to put me on the same rock? Eat me out until I can't move?"

He shakes his head. "No way. I just got your body temperature down. I'm not revving it up again. Rain check, though. I'd love to hear that lovely singing voice of yours one more time." He grins.

"You're lucky I'm sick." I aim to sound threatening. I sound like a kitten who's learning to purr.

"Aww, poor baby. Come here." Keston pulls me to his chest. "We'll get you back in the saddle soon." His voice is deep and husky. Like he's imagining yesterday at the waterfall.

I certainly am. I only have to peek at the sex rock and my clit jumps. It remembers better than me the feel of Keston's dangerous tongue lashing it around.

"Okay," I murmur. "I'll wait."

# Chapter Forty

The forest comes alive with bird song as evening approaches. Keston has kiss-tested my skin a million times to check my temperature. I had to stop thinking of how amazing sex with him would be to get my body heat to drop.

Once at the tiki hut, Keston insists that I sit under Prince

Harry while he pours *some* of the rum onto the pile of coconut branches and lights up the bonfire. He says he's saving the rest to create a special drink for me.

The dizziness I experienced earlier has faded. I'm on high alert for any possible aircraft in the sky that could spot our blazing bonfire.

I admire the way the fire crackles and spurts sparks into the night air. I may have passed out building it, but it's a beauty.

Keston adds bamboo stalks, coconut husks, and more branches to fan the flames. With the white foamy waves curling offshore, the sound of owls hooting in the night, and the scent of the coconut-fueled bonfire, the beach is a perfect romantic getaway spot.

Except for the stranded with no fresh clothes part.

I stare into the flames and pray for a plane or a cargo ship or anyone at all to see us.

"This was a great idea," Keston says, stacking more bamboo on the pyre. "Someone will surely see our smoke."

"I hope so."

The fire burns fast, sending dark grey plumes of smoke skyward. Keston squats next to me. We clasp hands watching the bonfire together.

Far off we hear rumbles of the approaching storm. It sounds like a distant train. But based on the clouds gathering and the waves roaring to shore, some scary weather thing is definitely coming.

I've never been in a hurricane or a tropical storm. Indoors or outdoors. I can tell from Keston's furrowed brows, it's not a joking around matter.

"We'll need to get to the interior before it hits," he says softly. "Find shelter."

I squeeze his hand. "We will."

I grab my stick and carve another tiny line into Prince Harry. Sunday is almost over.

Catching fish is out of the question in the dark. Keston roasts the second breadfruit and cuts it open to share for our meal.

"I'm sorry it isn't a better dinner." He hands me a leaf plate decorated with an architectural masterpiece made from cubed breadfruit.

"Are you kidding? You were busy saving my life."

"Twice," he smirks.

I've been avoiding thoughts of my almost drowning. Along with not going near the rocky end of the beach where that near-death experience occurred.

"After this is over, I'll need serious therapy. From a *real* therapist."

He tosses a tiny green coconut at my legs.

"Ungrateful wench."

I toss a tiny green coconut back at him. They lay around all over the beach waiting to sprout into new trees.

"This island is beautiful. If it weren't for being stuck here, it's refreshing to be disconnected from devices and get to know each other authentically." I can't believe I'm saying this. As if we're in a relationship. Which we are most definitely not.

"Glad you like it. I think it's perfect. Nature provides us with almost everything."

I smile at him. "We haven't been doing too badly, have we?"

"You've been amazing. I wouldn't have expected a queen bee like you to adapt so well."

I blush. "I know. Me either. The world-famous scientist Stephen Hawking said that intelligence is the ability to adapt to change."

He shrugs. "If you can't adapt you die."

I ponder his words.

"Wait until you see what else nature provides. Don't move."

I scoff. "I can't go anywhere."

While he's gone off on another pirate mission, I think about the ability to change one's life.

Everyone, not just me, avoids change. It's scary. It means going into an unknown situation with no idea of what can happen. Did I stay with Marcus for five years because it was familiar? Was I afraid to leave him? Is this misadventure some kind of cosmic wake-up call?

**K**eston reappears shirtless and sweaty per usual but holding a half coconut shell in his palm.

"I made something to cheer you up." His rakish grin eclipses the lines of worry he's worn all day.

"You mean to cheer *us* up!" I clap my hands. "Is this the famous drink?"

"Yes, and we only have one for now. So, we must share."

"*Pffft.*" I swat his arm as he sits next to me. "Don't I always?"

"Should I remind you of the Perrier water?"

I wave my hand. "That was before I knew you."

His eyebrows quirk up and down. "You mean before *I* knew *you*."

I have the nerve to blush.

"So, what's it called?" I change the subject.

"It's my version of a coconut daiquiri in a half shell. Taste."

He doesn't have to tell me twice. I raise the coconut shell to my mouth. I can tell he's rubbed the edges of the shell smooth, so I don't cut my lip.

I tilt the bowl and take a sip.

Sensations zing in my brain.

I take another sip. And another.

"So much for sharing," he laughs.

I lower the coconut shell. "You're a genius. What's in it?"

"My secret ingredient I put in the rum punches."

"Oh! Are you going to tell me your secret?"

"No."

"Come on. Who am I gonna tell?"

"If I tell you my secrets, you'll have to tell me yours."

"I'll think about it."

Meanwhile, I take another sip before passing the bowl to him. "What are you calling this drink?"

"Lime to My Coconut."

"That's perfect. So, it's got lime? And coconut? And rum . . ."

He clams up.

His profile is regal in the shadowy firelight. I poke his shoulder. "Tell me," I say in a whiney voice.

"Nope."

"How about we make it a game?" I suggest.

Keston looks up from examining his drink.

"What kind of game?" His eyes gleam.

We can call it, "*Never Have I Ever Told Anyone That . . .*"

Truth is, my secret is dying to be told. Who better to tell than someone I'll never see again? The deep desire to blurt it out scares me. But maybe if it's part of a game, it won't seem so overwhelming.

Besides, his secrets are probably more disturbing than mine. He's a playboy on an island of rich vacationers.

"You want to know my secrets?" he says.

"It's a game. You reveal a secret about yourself that you've never told a soul."

He frowns. "Why would I want to tell them to you?"

I pop a piece of leftover breadfruit from my leaf plate into my mouth. Its buttery texture melts on my tongue.

"Because we're stuck here. Once we're rescued, we'll probably never see each other again. And it'll be fun to discover stuff about each other no one else knows."

"We're never going to see each other again?"

"Probably."

He sits in silence. Like he's digesting more than just the roasted breadfruit cubes and coconut rum drink.

"Okay. You go first," he says, folding his leaf in half.

The rich coconut rum drink warms my belly. It also tinkers with my mind. I don't know if this is a game to play while under the influence of moonshine.

# Chapter Forty-One

"Fine. I'll start with a little secret. Never have I ever told anyone that I . . . once wanted to be a nun."

Keston hoots with laughter. Right in my ear.

I clap my hands over my ears.

"It's true. I was in fourth grade. My mom sent me to Catholic School. All my teachers were nuns. I loved them."

He stops laughing. Props an elbow on his bent knee and peers at me. "I can see you as a nun." His eyes rake up and down my near-naked body.

I push his elbow off his knee.

"Not very nun-like of you."

"Your turn. What's the secret ingredient in this delicious drink?" I eye the bottom of the coconut shell sadly.

"You must promise to keep my secret."

"Hold up. We forgot to pinkie swear." I hold out my pinkie finger.

He stares at it dumbfoundedly. "What's that?"

"Stick out your pinkie finger. We'll press our pinkies together. And promise not to share our secrets with anyone."

After we've signed our confidentiality agreement with a pinkie promise, the game continues.

"Okay. My secret rum punch ingredient and what I used today is a fruit most islanders take for granted. They leave them for the parrots to eat or let them drop and rot on the ground."

I listen intently. "Making use of a natural resource, I like it."

"It's called rough lemons."

"What lemons?"

He leans backward on his forearms because I'm hogging Prince Harry.

"I don't know if it has an official name. The fruit is a hybrid between a lime and an orange. It has the tart lime taste and the sweet orange taste. We call them rough lemons. They're larger than limes, greener than oranges."

"Whoa! And you found some here?"

"They grow all over."

"Amazing. Can you make more lime to my coconut drinks?"

"I could but we used up the rum on your bonfire."

"Damn!"

"I should have fed you the drink first."

"I'd have agreed to anything after that."

We laugh together.

"Your turn," he says, getting serious. "I want to know real secrets. Not ones from when you were eight."

I say the first thing that pops into my head that isn't the BIG secret.

"Never have I ever told anyone I don't like being a lawyer." I hesitate. It's the first time I've given words to the change I felt after making partner.

"Making partner was the big goal. It was a challenge. And I'm proud of my accomplishment. But after I made partner, it's become a chore to sign my own clients, as well as do all the casework."

This is a secret I didn't even know I was keeping from myself.

"I didn't know you were a lawyer," he says. "But it makes sense."

I don't dare touch that comment. "Okay, your turn."

I want to hurry and move on from this dangerous revelation. If I dwell on it, I'd need to implement changes and I've had enough of those for the year.

He gazes down the beach at the flames still licking the sky. "Never have I ever told a woman that I love her."

I blink. "Ever? You're in your thirties, dude."

"I would like to. It's never happened for me."

"Technically, that's not a secret."

He snorts. "It counts."

"Fine. Me again. Never have I ever told anyone that I want to be a stay-at-home Mom if I have kids. Everyone assumes I'd go back to work as a lawyer."

"I see a pattern here," he grins.

"What pattern?"

"You want to change careers."

I cover my face with my hands.

He scoots closer. I inch over to give him space against Prince Harry.

He takes my hand in his big rough one. "It's okay to want to change your life."

"Wanting to and doing it are not the same thing."

"Never have I ever told anyone that I want to open my own bar one day."

"You do?" I ask surprised. "I thought you were happy being a bartender at the resort."

"I'm happy there. But I see a bar on the beach with surfboards, live reggae bands, and spicy cocktails. They won't let me use habanero peppers in the resort drinks."

"Spicy cocktails. Sounds like someplace I'd love."

"One day."

"Yes, one day I'll stop being a lawyer. And you'll have your own bar.

# Chapter Forty-Two

"I have a bigger secret." I'm not sure if I'm preparing him or myself.

He puts an arm around my shoulders. It's comforting and safe and the perfect place to reveal the event that changed my life.

"I have a daughter," I blurt out.

I feel his body stiffen a tiny bit. "Go on," he says.

I swallow hard. Clench my hands into fists to stay seated and not get up and run away. The beat of my heart is louder than the waves drumming on the shore.

"I was twenty-one years old. A junior in college. I don't know who the father is."

I drop my face in my hands. "I'm so ashamed to say I don't know."

"What happened?"

"I'd been sheltered. Catholic School all the way until I graduated high school. A mother who micromanaged my life. When I got to college, I partied as much as I studied. Or more."

"Like most kids, I bet."

"Yes, but I slept with quite a few guys."

"You make it sound illegal. I heard that's college life."

"Until I got pregnant. I remember the day I found out. I'd been sick for weeks. Thought it was a bad cold. The college health clinic ran tests. I learned it wasn't a bad cold, it was a baby."

"Wow."

"I was so scared. All I could think was, my mother will kill me."

"What about your friends?"

I shake my head hard against his shoulder. "I was a chicken. I pretended I was fine and wore baggy clothing for most of the semester."

"You had her by yourself?"

"I was in so much denial that I let weeks go by and didn't do anything. I decided to find her a nice family and signed with an adoption agency that handles cases like mine. College girls getting pregnant. There's a whole business for that."

"Lord, CJ, that was major to do alone."

"I had her after summer vacation started. I was an intern at a law firm. I took a week off work and went back as if nothing happened. No one knew I was pregnant because I wore very blousy dresses. At least I don't think anyone knew. It's scary how easy it was to hide."

Something about Keston Kips. Once I start talking, I can't seem to stop. It's like the first night we met when I told him about my breakup.

"She'll be nineteen years old this summer. I think about her every day. And I believe the reason none of my relationships work out with men is because of that. Bad karma. For giving away my child. For not knowing who her father is. For being too afraid to tell my mother or anyone else that I was pregnant."

My voice drops to a whisper. "I don't deserve a loving relationship after what I did."

Keston wraps both arms around me. "It's easy to look back and blame our younger selves for stuff we did or didn't do at *that* time in our lives. That twenty-one-year-old girl in college was scared and alone. She did the best she knew how. And she needs you to be proud of her. Because she's hurting that you aren't."

I lean back and stare deeply into Keston's eyes. "Thank you."

His eyes flit over my face. "You're welcome."

I lean against his chest and sigh. "I thought of looking for her. But I realized it's not fair to her. Or her family."

"Maybe one day she'll find you."

"Yeah, maybe."

"I've got a secret."

I sit up and dry my eyes. "Tell me."

"Never have I ever told anyone that I want to kiss *you*." He points to me in case there's any confusion.

"What the hell! You've been kissing me all day. On my cheek. My forehead, even my lips."

"Not for *medical* purposes. A real kiss."

I circle my hand in the air. "Well, get on with it, mister."

Before I finish that sentence, Keston's lips are on mine. Powerful, hungry, and tender all at the same time.

His tongue teases open my lips. Probes its way into my mouth. Then in a move I wasn't expecting, he lifts me off the sand and sets me on his lap, legs on either side of his waist.

A bulge the size of the Grand Tetons fills his shorts. It jabs me in my most tender spot.

"You taste delicious," he says.

"I've been brushing my teeth with a piece of bamboo and lime."

His laugh is throaty. "You definitely know how to adapt."

"I'm trying," I say as I squirm against his growing shaft.

# Chapter Forty-Three

**K**eston and I fall asleep wrapped in each other's arms. Not because we had sex. He's saving his condom for the right moment. Which wasn't last night with me feeling vulnerable about my daughter, and him worrying my body temperature would rise.

I thought we'd have more time to make love in the morning.

After the drama of secrets and the scare of my heat stroke subsided.

As soon as my eyes pop open, I know today will be different. And not in a good way. What woke me was a noise. A cross between a plane's engines taking off and heavy bass from speakers at a frat party.

Our lovely tiki hut is tearing apart before my eyes. Branches that we weaved together flap up and down wildly. Some tear loose and fly into the sky. Like paper airplanes.

I crawl out and stand up. I'm almost blown back down.

What the hell! I can barely walk. The wind pushes me back with every step forward. It reminds me of trying to swim against the current.

The force of the wind sends the sand swirling and blowing everywhere. Including right into my eyes.

I blink hard. Try to clear the grains of sand from my eyeballs.

I drop to all fours and crawl to make progress.

The coconut trees bend almost in half, their branches sweeping the sand. Coconuts drop around me as the wind shakes the trees like a giant with a grudge.

"Keston!" I shout into the wind. His name echoes back to me.

It's useless.

I gaze around at the waves walloping the shore. The sandstorm swirls dangerously close. The trees and coconuts that once fed and protected us are now weapons in the open space.

The last thing I need is to get hit by a flying coconut! But I can't leave without Keston. And I don't know where to go.

The waterfall. Maybe he's there. He goes there first thing to fill up our two water bottles.

A loud clap of thunder reverberates in the thick air. Lightning streaks across the sky almost instantly after the thunder.

From what I recall about weather, you can count how far away the storm is based on the number of seconds between the thunder and the lightning.

One second between thunder and lightning means one mile away. Two seconds means two miles away.

But this is zero seconds. Thunder booms. Lightning bolts split the sky simultaneously.

It's from a flash of lightning that I see Keston. He's standing by the tiki hut, frantically tossing branches aside, yelling my name. I can't hear him. I only see his mouth moving. But it looks as if he's shouting, "CJ!"

"Over here," I wave my arms. Sand grits its way into my mouth.

He doesn't see me.

I close my eyes and crawl in the direction of the hut.

Suddenly, a pair of strong arms grip me. "We must go. Now!"

"Duh!" I want to say. But I don't dare open my mouth again.

With our arms wrapped around each other's waists to stay together, we stagger toward the forest.

It's a bit quieter than the beach. But the storm is huffing and puffing and blowing our proverbial door down.

From up high, tree branches slam down around us. Keston and I move as one, leaping, dodging, faking side to side like football players outwitting the opposing team. In this case, the hurricane is the other side.

Keston stops running. Adjusts the beach bag and dry bag strapped across his body.

I'm panting like a dog after a hard run. My heart slams against my chest. I press a hand to slow it down.

*Deep breaths. Take deep breaths to center yourself.*

"What the hell is happening?" I cry. "Is this a real hurricane?"

The monster-sized trees block out the light. It's as dark as night in the middle of the forest. I can't see his facial expression.

"This shouldn't be happening. We don't get storms like this in the dry season," Keston shouts.

All I'm thinking is that I'm not prepared for this. I don't have any training. I haven't read any articles or how-to guides on surviving a storm. I don't have the right clothes to endure a rainy superstorm.

"Are we going to die?" I wring my hands.

Keston grips my shoulders. "No!" He shouts. "We must stay alive. Whatever it takes."

I nod hard, tears mixing with the rainwater gushing in rivulets from bent leaves. The rain turns the forest floor into a carpet of deep mud. It sucks my flip flops down, making it difficult to lift my legs.

Keston has already tossed his slippers. He can move faster and quicker now.

I'm the one holding us back. But I can't shun the only barrier between me and every creepy crawly down there.

I gaze at my feet in horror at the dark mud caking my ankles.

This is a nightmare. One I'm not sure I'll survive.

"We have to find shelter," Keston says. "The hillside behind the waterfall is too slippery to climb and we'll be exposed up there."

Thunder resounds in the air. Lightning cracks across the sky, revealing the canopy of trees that are falling like dominos around us.

"Come on." Keston grips my hand tightly.

I can't lift my foot out of the mud.

At that moment, a loud crash splinters the air. A dark shape descends upon us. The sky is falling. Literally.

Keston pushes me hard. I fall in a heap of mud. The dark shape lands with a sickening crunch.

Screams echo through the jungle. Not mine.

Loud. Painful. Screams. Like an animal dying.

I can't see a thing. Wet leaves cover my face.

Shock and dread fill me. I can't move a muscle. I'm lying under branches, water dripping in my eyes, mud up to my thighs.

"CJ," Keston's pained voice filters through my shock.

"Keston, are you okay?"

"Go to the silk cotton tree."

"What?" I blubber.

"Silk cotton tree." His breath is labored and strange. A gurgling sound.

"Get to the tree. It's straight ahead."

My heart is being ripped out at the sound of his agony as he struggles to speak.

They say you don't know what you're made of until you're under extreme stress. Your true character emerges. Surviving the heartbreak of giving up my daughter was tough. Surviving on a deserted island for a few days was hard.

But this disaster right here? It's on a whole different level.

It's sink or swim. Literally.

A fire lights my insides.

It's time to move my ass.

# Chapter Forty-Four

Jolts of hardcore adrenaline surge through my veins. I push leaves and branches aside like a mad woman.

Once clear of the branches that covered me, I assess the situation. I don't have any light, so I feel my way across the massive tree that fell on us.

I listen for Keston's breathing. I climb over the tree in that direction.

"CJ."

"I'm coming. Hold on."

"No, go to safety."

"I will. Keep talking to me so I can find you."

His breathing is shallow.

"Don't die," I yell. "I'll kill you."

A faint wheezing sound comes from the far side. I tread over branches carefully. Finally, I reach the edge of the tree. It's so big that even toppled over, it is six feet high sideways.

"Hey, I forgot to tell you a secret."

"What?" his voice is weaker.

"Once I find you and we're safe, I'll tell you."

"Okay."

The sound of his voice leads me to him.

I gasp.

The tree has landed on his leg. I can't see his face or upper body as I'm on the other side of the tree.

I bite my lip. No time to be weak and cry and complain.

"Hey Keston, honey. I need the beach bag. Can you push it out from under all those crazy leaves?"

His soft grunt of pain is the only response. But I hear something being pushed on the ground.

Patting the slimy, wet leaves, I feel the bag and pull it toward me. My phone is in its waterproof case. I take it out and turn it on. The battery is working. I shine the light on the tree.

Rain slashes against my face. It pours from the opening in the forest canopy left behind by the fallen tree.

I swipe rain from my eyes and hold the phone steady. My stomach turns at the blood on the ground. If I don't move fast, Keston will die.

"You promised me a good time, Keston. I'm holding you to it. We still have that condom, baby. It's for me. Don't you forget it."

A faint chuckle reaches my ears.

"CJ."

"Yes, honey. I'm here."

Thunder roars its mighty voice. Lightning illuminates the sky, showing me everything I need to see.

The crashing sound of another tree falling in the storm makes me jump.

*Focus CJ. No time to panic.*

His leg is trapped. Not his entire body, thank God. The tree is at an angle. Half its length lays across a massive rock. The other half is on the forest floor. Keston is under a branch the size of a whole tree.

If he hadn't pushed me out of the way, this would be me now. Keston saved my life a third time.

I sit on the edge of the rock shelf the tree is on to think. I must save his life. It's not even a question.

But how can I get Keston out from under that branch? How can I see in the dark to do anything? How can I move him if I get him out? Where will we go if he can't walk? How much blood has he lost? Will I make things worse by moving the tree branch? Suppose it's stopping an artery of blood from gushing, and he dies.

Fuck!

Fear tugs at my soul. Trying to get me to quit. To say this is impossible. Give up and cry.

But I refuse to give in.

Fear is nothing but a bully. You must give fear a swift kick in the butt when it's needed.

"Okay, baby," I shout with fake confidence. "Here's what we're gonna do."

# Chapter Forty-Five

The tree branches scratch my legs and arms as I climb over them to reach Keston. My heart drops when I see him lying there helpless and unconscious.

His face and upper body are covered with mud. I try to wipe it away, but my own hands are dirty, so it doesn't help.

Leaning over his body I listen for his breath.

Fear grips my heart. I know CPR. I'm ready to do it if I must.

"You'll be okay," I tell him although he can't hear me.

The rain and wind cease. It's eerily quiet. Like the storm has passed. This must be what meteorologists call the eye of the storm.

I shine the phone light along the ground to see where the tree hit him, what's broken, and where to start digging.

Because that's what I've decided to do.

Me, the woman afraid of every slimy creepy crawly thing under the sun, I'm going to dig through this mud until I scoop out enough dirt around his leg to get him out.

I prop up my phone with the light facing the ground. I take a deep breath and stick my hands in the earth.

I pull out handfuls of dirt and toss it aside. The dirt clings to my fingers. I shake it off and stick my hands back into the deep, dark mud.

Don't think about it. Think about something else. Something wonderful.

I imagine a scene where Keston and I are laughing and sipping cocktails at his own beach bar surrounded by friends.

I'm wearing a floaty white dress with flowers around the hem. He's shaking up drinks. His new flavor, lime to my coconut, is a big hit.

I can taste the sweet-sour flavor of the rough lemons mixing with the creamy coconut and the island rum. So cold and delicious, it hits just right.

People are asking for more. Keston's handsome face shows love for everyone. He listens to their problems. Gives the best advice. Then pours out their drinks. Giving them a taste of paradise. A cute bar sign reads, *"The Doc is in."* A gift from me as a memento of how we met.

He circles around to where I'm seated. Kisses my cheek.

Plucks me off my stool for a dance to the soulful reggae tune blaring over the speakers. Or maybe a band. Yes, he wants live music.

We're happy. We dance and he twirls me around and around.

It's a sublime evening.

"Owww," the sound of Keston's voice snaps me out of my trance. I look down and realize I've dug away a lot of dirt and leaves. Keston's leg is exposed. I can't see too clearly but I need to move quickly.

I scoot around to his shoulders. "Kes, I have to drag you out. Keep your leg as still as possible. Do not bend it."

I reach under his shoulders, but I can't move him. When I tug on his body, he screams in pain. It's unbearable.

Rain starts falling again. The wind has resumed. It's worse than before. Objects are flying about.

I push my dripping hair out of my eyes.

I search around the area frantically. I need to find a piece of wood to splint his leg, so it won't move.

I strip off my dress and begin tearing crocheted pieces apart. A large branch falls near my head. I scream and leap back.

If I don't move fast, we'll both die.

Think of something powerful. Inspirational.

Harriet Tubman comes to mind. I don't know why. She just does. I think about her journeys from the southern states to the north over and over rescuing all those enslaved people. She must have had many nights in swamps and mud. She must have dug in the earth a bunch of times to rescue men, women, and children. I'm sure she built splints. She was a rescuer.

I only have to do it once.

Just this once.

With that thought in mind, I grab the best-sized wood I can find and get to work strapping it to Keston's leg. Tying my dress strips as tightly as possible. I seem to have more strength than ever.

"Thank you," I whisper when I've secured his leg. "Now, please help me move him safely."

"I love you, CJ."

"What?" I'm sure I didn't hear right. Keston must be delirious.

"You got this," I tell myself.

I grip his broad shoulders and pull as gently as possible.

He's a large man. He doesn't budge.

I bow my head and pray.

I've done everything right. I can do this part too.

I close my eyes and pull Keston Kips' shoulders. He feels lighter somehow. I pull firmly. He budges a tiny bit.

I pull again. He's even lighter now.

I smile. I'm not alone. I pull again and this time I slide Keston out from the hole and away from the tree.

I hear the applause in my head. It's me clapping for myself.

# Chapter Forty-Six

Once I get him out and he opens his eyes, I feel as if nothing can stop us now. Although he's in excruciating pain, he leans on my shoulder as we hop, limp, and drag ourselves to the gigantic silk cotton tree he'd seen a short distance away before he was hit by the falling tree.

Keston was right about the silk cotton tree. It could house

and protect an entire family. Its roots rise at least ten feet high out of the ground and curve in a way that allows us to step inside the tree as if we're stepping inside a wooden castle.

"Wow!" I exclaim. "A genuine treehouse."

I help Keston lay down on the soft dry ground. Within the protection of the silk cotton tree's roots, we can't see the storm raging outside but we can still hear it.

Keston's face has been washed clean by the rain. So are my arms and legs. I no longer have a dress. I'm cold and shivering.

"Body heat is the best," he says through chattering teeth.

"I've heard." I lay down next to Keston. Put my arms around him. To keep us both as warm as possible.

"Just don't die on me. I need to learn how to make that drink."

He gurgles a laugh.

"And from now on, no matter where I go, I'm taking a rain jacket with me. In my backpack, my briefcase, or rolled up in a dry bag."

After witnessing the practical benefits of Keston's dry bag, including how it's protecting my book, I'm committed to using them as a daily accessory.

Once I've warmed up a bit, I turn my light on Keston's leg. He's drifting in and out of sleep. I examine it carefully. I have no medical training, but I can see a bone protruding. Before today, I'd have fainted. Or turned my face away and hid my eyes.

Now, I look it over. I'm careful not to touch or jostle it. The blood has stopped thank goodness. The crocheted dress really came in handy. Its strong ties are holding his leg together nicely. Who would have thought?

"Come lie down."

Keston's voice is weak. I screw open a bottle of water and hold his head up so he can drink. Then I rest his head in my lap as I lean against the strong roots of this beautiful tree. I stroke his curls and touch his ears.

His breathing evens out and he drifts to sleep.

In another world and time, I could see us together. Married even. With kids, a home, and a deep lasting love based on mutual respect and being our authentic selves.

"Yes, Keston Kips, if my life were different, I'd have chosen *you.*"

He groans in his sleep. I press my fingers to his wrist to check his pulse.

We're out of immediate danger. But Keston needs medical care.

I slide open my phone and start sending SOS messages. I leave my phone on. Hoping to hear something back.

It didn't work on the beach. But we're on a different part of the island now. We deserve a miracle.

# Chapter Forty-Seven

**M**y first thought when I open my eyes is Keston. Not my sore arms that feel as if elephants are playing tug of war with them.

Not my aching neck from sleeping sitting up against hard tree roots. Not my stomach growling like an angry animal. Not even my lack of clothing.

"Kes, honey, are you okay?" I touch his forehead. His head is still resting on my lap. He's burning with fever. Shaking from head to toe. Most likely with the chills that accompany a fever.

My phone's battery is in the red, but it's holding on to its last charge.

Outside our haven, the rolling thunder has stopped. Silence never sounded so sweet.

I ease Keston's head off my lap. I have to get us off this island today. I bow my head and whisper a prayer.

"Whoever's in charge up there, listen up. We need help and we need it now."

I don't think demanding help is the way to go about it, but with all that's been happening to us, a harsh plea is necessary.

And that's when I hear it.

Or don't hear it.

I cock my ear to the opening of the tree. "No way."

"Kes!" I shout. "I hear something."

A groan is all he can manage. Biting my lip, I check his wound. His leg is turning a funny color. My heart drops.

I scramble to step outside the tree.

I inhale sharply. A world of sparkling greenery greets me.

The piece of sky I can see is blue and cloudless. The standing trees wave their polished green leaves about as if cheering for their survival.

Pairs of green parrots flit from branch to branch, chattering loudly. Flowers shine in all their multi-colored glory. Lavender blossoms fall at my feet. The same lavender flowers that grew on the trees surrounding the waterfall.

The entire forest is teeming with life. In sharp contrast to the terror of yesterday.

If a Disney movie came to life, this would be it. I'm standing in the middle of a jungle, where the trees and plants, flowering bushes, and hidden creatures are rejoicing. I'm just a guest.

Okay, enough of this. I must find the source of that noise.

It wasn't a jungle noise. Or a beach noise. It was a man-made whirring. I heard it at the resort. When the landscapers were clearing the grounds.

My ears perk up. I hear it again.

"Oh my God! It's a weed wacker."

I heard it outside the villa. I heard it while driving my golf cart around the resort. I thought how annoying it was that they couldn't make those things operate silently. They were ruining paradise.

In my delirious state, I shout inside the silk cotton tree. "Kes, we're going to be rescued. The weed wackers are coming!"

Then I tell the forest, "It's okay. I won't let them cut you down. Just make a teeny tiny path to rescue Keston."

The trees wave their branches back at me. As if saying, "we understand."

So, this is what people call communing with nature.

I race inside and kiss Keston on his forehead. Beads of perspiration run down his face. He tries to grip my hand but fails.

"I'll be back."

I grab my phone, my beach bag, and his dry bag. I stop outside the tree and take a deep calming breath.

How will I find my way to the beach? More importantly, how will I find my way back here?

Lavender petals catch my eye.

They aren't easy to pick up but I scoop as many as I can into my beach bag.

Then, walking in the direction I think we came from, I drop lavender petals behind me, to mark my path. When I pass the poor tree that tumbled on Keston, I know I'm going the right way.

I listen intently. For the sound of the weed wackers, the waterfall, or the waves. I recall Keston saying I can't get lost if I can hear the surf breaking.

The walk is strenuous on my sore muscles. I climb over many fallen soldiers. I pat their trunks sadly. This climate change storm destroyed a lot of beauty. I make a mental promise to the forest to help replant more trees.

Moving onward is the only thing I can do. If I stop and rest, I won't be able to get back up. That's how much everything hurts.

The sound of the waterfall is sweetly familiar. I'm almost out of petals, but I know the way to the beach from there.

Parting the tree branches, I step into the clearing where I had the best sexual experience of my life. On a damn rock.

The water flow over the high bank is a muddy brown color. The pool is mucky. Erosion from the storm has brought down a lot of dirt and debris.

It means I can't refill my water bottle. I trudge on thirsty and sticky with the humidity. This day has got to get better.

# Chapter Forty-Eight

When I emerge on the beach, my skin is scratched up and sweaty. I run straight to the calm blue sea, arms outstretched, and dive in.

Such a relief.

I dive down, touch the sand and pop back up. I wring out

my hair as I stride through the waves back to sand. That's when I notice it.

Prince Harry has been torn right out of the sand and is laying like a corpse on the beach. The tiki hut is no more. I run to the tree.

"No. Not you too."

I sink down onto the trunk of the once beautiful swaying palm tree that allowed me to rest against its trunk when I was tired, sick, and grouchy. Tears fall for the first time since this storm started.

Some might say, it's just a tree. But they'd be wrong. It was alive. It was my friend.

I swallow against the lump in my throat.

If I'm going to rescue Keston, I'd better get a move on.

I walk up and down the beach. Searching for whatever made that whirring noise.

It's when I reach the rocky end that I hear it again. But it's not a weed wacker. It's a helicopter. Flying over the island. It's moving slowly as if searching for something. As if searching for us!

The black metal bird dips low over the middle of the island. It flies upward then circles around and drops low again.

I hurry and grab one of Prince Harry's palm branches. Sand kicks up behind me as I near the rocks waving the branch high.

The lighter is at the bottom of Keston's dry bag. Once I reach the highest rock, I shake the lighter out, flick it open, and ignite the branch like a pro, unafraid of burning my fingers.

The branch flares beautifully.

Jumping up and down on the rocks, ignoring the pain in my bare feet, I wave the burning branch left and right. I spin in a circle. I shout at the top of my lungs. I don't know what else to do to get the helicopter's attention.

As my branch fire dwindles, I panic. The helicopter rises high in the sky. It's swooping away.

"Come back!" I cry from a throat hoarse with shouting.

I scramble back down the rocks. Prince Harry is the closest tree to the shore now that it has fallen over and is lying across the sand.

Tears stream down my face. I run around piling up Prince Harry's branches that the sun has dried out.

I peel off my swimsuit, also dry from the intense sun, and add it to the pile. I look around. What else can I burn?

In a frenzy, I rip the pages out of my romance novel, dropping them on top of the swimsuit and branches. When the fire catches, I blow on the flames and fan them. Like Keston taught me.

"Come on, Prince Harry! Come on Kennedy Ryan. Come on Versace."

A mother of all blazes flares up. Smoke plumes fill the sky. I dance around the fire like a woman gone mad.

I leap. I holler. I wave my fists at the sky.

They must see me now. They must hear me now.

I am not invisible. I won't be silenced.

The whirring noise is first. Then, the helicopter reappears in the sky. Coming from behind the island.

I cheer and run across the sand to meet it.

Like a demure lady spreading her dress before she sits, the metal bird lowers itself carefully onto the sand.

Two men jump out.

One is a medic holding a backpack marked with a red cross. My heart soars.

The other has broad shoulders. Dark glossy skin. Immaculate linen shirt.

"Marcus!" I stagger toward my ex. "You came."

"Of course, I came. I got your SOS. I still have you on Find My Friends."

"But . . . I have no service. And I . . ." This is not the time to tell him I deleted his phone number.

"I have the latest technology on my phone. You never blocked me on the app. I tracked you from satellites. I had to wait until the hurricane blew over before we could fly to the island."

"I can't believe you came to rescue me."

"Carmela, what happened to your clothes?"

I glance down. I'm wearing absolutely nothing. My swimsuit is in tatters. My beach dress is now an emergency bandage. My body is covered from head to toe with black soot and sand. It's a wonder he recognized me.

His shocked expression is not his fault.

"Who cares about my clothes, Marcus? We have to save Keston."

<h1 style="text-align:center">Chapter Forty-Nine</h1>

Everything from there on feels like a movie. The helicopter is a fully equipped Medivac hired by Marcus to rescue me.

When I explain that Keston is in the rainforest with a broken leg, the paramedic and pilot, who is also an EMT, rush into rescue mode. They gather supplies and a stretcher.

Marcus gives me the shirt off his back. Literally. He can't do anything about shoes, so I walk barefoot across the sand leading the three-man crew.

"Follow me," I say, directing them on the now familiar route to the waterfall.

Not even five minutes into the walk, as we dodge hanging branches, and squish through mud and debris, me with no shoes on, Marcus exclaims, "I can't believe you've survived in here for days."

The paramedics make noises like they're equally surprised.

"Carmela, you can't tolerate New York City pigeons."

"Ugh," I shiver in disgust. "They're nasty."

"Right," he mutters. "And *this* isn't?"

"If I could come in my own boat with a picnic and a bottle of champagne. This would be a true paradise."

I can picture it well.

I push aside hanging vines to reveal the waterfall. The water is less muddy. Time is passing and we're taking too long to get to Keston.

"Hurry up," I urge.

Adrenaline pushes me to jog over rocks and tree limbs.

"Be careful," Marcus calls out. Like I'm a child or a helpless creature.

It's a good thing he can't see my eye roll.

In all the days Kes and I were stuck here, he never once told me to '*be careful*.' It came with the territory that we'd have to be careful.

From the waterfall, I scan the ground for the lavender petals. They're like tiny beacons of light marking the way to the silk cotton tree.

"Are you following the pink petals?" Marcus asks incredulously.

"It's lavender."

"They're from the jacaranda trees, miss," the pilot, Paul, says. "They grow on our island too."

"You're from St. Nicholas?" I ask.

"Yes, when your husband called last night to tell us you sent emergency signals from No Man's Land, we prepared the helicopter to come as soon as we could. I'm sorry we couldn't come earlier."

I ignore the husband part and say, "It's okay. We had a hurricane going on. How is St. Nicholas?"

He shakes his head. "They've started cleaning up. It's a mess. Some injured folks. No fatalities, thank goodness."

"Thank goodness." I cross my fingers.

"This is where he got hit," I point out the fallen tree to the men. Their faces are grim when they see the size of the tree.

I describe the ordeal of getting Keston out from under it.

Marcus's skeptical expression says he can't believe my story.

Doesn't matter. Because we arrive at the silk cotton tree. It's bigger in the daylight. A giant of a tree, with roots that spread vertically and horizontally.

Marcus's eyes widen. So do the paramedics.

"Come on." I duck into the giant roots. It's like passing through a magic door.

"Keston?" I call softly.

The paramedics push past me and drop to their knees next to his body. There is no movement. No sound. Nothing.

I clap my hands over my mouth to hold back my scream.

# Chapter Fifty

arcus springs into action. He takes out a satellite phone and calls ahead to the hospital on St. Nicholas. He tells them to have an ambulance waiting at the airstrip.

"He's not dead, is he?" I'm so scared I'll scream that I'm still covering my mouth with my hands.

"He would be in about a half hour," Paul says morbidly. "He's one lucky man to have you with him. You saved his life."

I feel no relief at those words. We're not out of the woods yet.

But there's nothing more I can do. Keston Kips' life is out of my hands now.

My shoulders shake. My chin wobbles. I hiccup to hold back my tears.

Marcus puts an arm around me. As the two paramedics walk by with Keston strapped to the stretcher, I reach out and touch Keston's hand.

"I'll be right behind you."

I feel a slight pressure on my hand.

I do not want to let him go.

The hardest thing I'm forced to do is walk behind that stretcher. And pretend I'm not in love with Keston Kips.

# Chapter Fifty-One

**D**ay one without Keston.

How can being apart from someone you've known only a few days hurt like this? But being apart from Keston feels as if the universe has ripped out a piece of my soul. I can't sleep, eat, or stop crying as I wait in my villa for news about his surgeries.

The doctors examined me at Marcus's insistence. I'm fine. Physically.

They sent me back to the villa with a hydration pack and Advil. Told me to rest and call them if anything comes up.

I'd have liked a room next to Keston's, but that wasn't an option.

He's had to undergo a few procedures to rectify the damage done to his leg.

Marcus is paying for Keston's surgeries. Even though it's a free hospital. With decent medical care. Marcus is flying in the best surgeons.

I asked him to do it. I would have begged.

I originally wanted to air vac Keston to a stateside hospital. Unfortunately, without a visa, the paperwork would take too long to organize.

Hence, the surgeons arriving by private plane in less time than it takes to set up the operating rooms.

Marcus says he's doing it to say thank you to the man who kept me safe on the island. I'm just grateful. Whatever the reason.

It's a sit-and-wait situation.

D*ay two without Keston.*
I can't sleep. I pace the carpets. They're too soft.
The bed is too big.
The pillows too puffy.
The espresso too strong.
Everything is too much.
Nothing feels right.

I find myself taking deep breath after deep breath. But it doesn't slow down my racing heart.

Marcus is staying in another villa at the resort after I reminded him that we broke up.

I know, *Ouch!* But I'm speaking my truth. No longer trying to be the good, accommodating woman for him.

The more I pull back, the more he reaches. Like we're players who've switched sides on the court.

D ay three without Keston.

Bubbles float on the steaming water reaching my chin. I've been soaking in the villa's giant tub for an hour. Refilling the hot water several times. I stare out the windows at the beach in the distance.

My mind is a merry-go-round of questions.

How is Keston doing?

Has he come out of the surgeries?

Is he in pain?

Does he miss me like I miss him?

The loofah is an island floating on the water.

I've scrubbed my skin as hard as I can. Grains of sand invade every crevice. The more I wash away, the more there is.

No Man's Land insists on being a physical part of me.

It's already an emotional and mental chunk of my being.

The hours crawl by.

Marcus is still on the island in his villa working remotely. He says he's not leaving without me.

Finally, I get a call from the hospital.

Technically, only Keston's family is supposed to be

informed about his surgery results, but they feel sorry for me. I've been calling every hour.

"Out of danger."

My heartbeat soars at those words.

"Can I come down to see him?" I ask.

"No, he's resting. It's better if you rest too."

I hang up and go outside on the patio. I have a few words of thanks to utter to the Universe.

# Chapter Fifty-Two

My family and friends have been texting, asking for updates on my ordeal of being stranded on an island and surviving a hurricane.

It's difficult to separate the ordeal of being stranded and living through a hurricane from the exhilaration of falling in love. They happened at the same time. The love grew despite the disasters. Or maybe *because* of them.

My text messages are brief but filled with gratitude for their concern and love.

They respond with warm wishes to get back to normal as soon as possible. To put it behind me and move on. My mom on video chat expresses how happy she is that Marcus and I have reconciled.

"It's good to see you making wise choices again," Mom says.

Not wanting to burst her bubble, or get into an argument, I smile and nod.

Everyone's behaving as if getting back to "normal" is the goal.

I don't know what normal is any more.

Isolation and near-death experiences can change a person's outlook.

I stir the water in my tub. Another bath. Another day of feeling as if I'm covered with mud.

I slide my head under the bubbles and lay there holding my breath for as long as I can.

When my lungs ache to bursting, I pop up. It's a game I play. How long can I stay under the water before I must come up to breathe?

I'm not sure if I'm testing my survival skills. Or if near-death experiences are my new norm.

I wish I could talk to Keston.

<h1 style="text-align:center">Chapter Fifty-Three</h1>

After almost a week of staying up all night, sleepless and exhausted, Marcus insists we fly home to New York.

"You can see a doctor there."

"The doctors said I was fine," I push back.

"Not that kind of doctor."

"Oh, you mean a counselor. A therapist." If he only knew I wanted one after we broke up. To try and understand what was wrong with me.

"Nothing is wrong with me," I tell him. "I'll get through this."

I got through a lot already. Without him.

Marcus nods. His eyes are full of concern. A Marcus I've never seen before.

"Do you know Prince Harry died to save Keston?"

"What?"

"Everything happens for a reason."

"I want to help you, Carmela."

"Then take me to the hospital. I'm not leaving without saying goodbye to Keston."

He frowns. "I don't believe he's allowed visitors other than family right now."

I sit, feet tucked under me, chin resting on my hands. "I'll wait then."

The hospital floors are scrubbed clean. The smell of antiseptic invades my nostrils. Bright lights shine down on me like fake sunshine.

At the door to Keston's room, I stop. My sundress flares out as the ceiling fan blows its fake wind on me.

I rap on the door. Before I turn the doorknob, I slide on my sunglasses. To hide the dark circles under my eyes. We haven't seen each other for five days. It feels like five years.

I'm a little bit frightened to face Keston in this environment. The memory of what we did. What he did to me. How I felt with him. It all seems like a story we read together. Not like something that happened.

That's why I need to see him. To know that it did. And that what I feel is real.

Keston turns his head slowly. He watches me walk towards his bed. The usual smiley, charming, carefree man is gone. In the bed is a solemn, serious one.

"Hi, there," I whisper. "Can I sit?"

He indicates a chair next to his bed.

"How are you?"

"Better. Recovering. Bored."

I yank off the sunglasses and fold them away. "I brought you a present." I reach into my bag and take out a book. One of the many I brought on my trip. "I think you may like this one. It's another romance novel."

A smile inches up his lips. "What happened to our other couple?"

"They got burned."

His eyebrows hunch. "Couldn't stand the heat, huh?"

"Yeah, well you know what they say."

He holds the book close to his chest. "What?"

"Don't play with fire if you can't handle the flame."

A low chuckle escapes his lips. "I missed you, CJ."

Finally.

"I missed you too, Keston."

I'm about to say a lot more, but he holds up a hand.

"Marcus came to visit me yesterday."

My back arches. "He did? Why?"

"Wanted to know what happened between us on the island."

"I hope you told him the truth."

Keston looks at his leg strung up in a cast. Shakes his head. "He helped to save my life on the island. If it weren't for him, I'd have lost my leg. The medical team he brought in saved it. He really loves you."

*But do you love me?*

I bite the words back.

"Did he say anything else?"

"Only that you are going back to New York this weekend."

He slides open the bedside drawer. His hand rummages around inside before pulling out the white shell necklace he always wore.

"I wish I had something better to give you to say thank you. For everything. Especially for saving my life. I don't know how you got me out from under that tree, CJ."

This is not going how I imagined. I expected us to throw ourselves at each other. Or at least I'd throw myself into his arms.

We'd seal our love with kisses and cuddles. I'd climb into the hospital bed next to him like they do in the movies and TV shows.

The necklace swings from his fingers. I reach over and take it. Our fingers touch and static electricity zips through me.

"Are you saying goodbye to me?" I ask.

I'm struggling to think of how to change the course of this conversation. It's heading for the cliffs.

"CJ, I'm happy we met. It wasn't under the best conditions. But I'll never forget you."

Why is he sounding so cold? So aloof? Where is the passionate man who took me to great heights on a rock? Fed me bananas? Massaged me with plant gel to protect my skin?

Whose massively hard cock rubbed against my pussy until I exploded on his lap? Where did he go?

If this is normal life, I don't want it.

I want what we had. I can't tell him that. He's recovering. The last thing he needs is a lovesick older woman moaning she needs another orgasm. From his lips. His hands. His cock.

Okay, that's not *all* I want from him. But it's clear he doesn't feel the same way about me. Not one bit.

"So, this is it?" I smooth down my dress.

He grabs my hand. The warmth of his touch feels like home.

"You're the only person in the world who knows everything about me," I choke up.

"I hope you share more of yourself with others. You're too special to hide behind secrets."

Tears threaten to fall. I suck them up and try to be brave. I couldn't speak if I wanted to. He's not hearing me say goodbye. Like what we shared was a fling.

His eyes glisten.

"Why are you being this way?" I cry, wringing my hands.

He takes a deep breath.

"You live an amazing life, CJ. I'm a bartender living a simple life on a small island. I cannot see myself in a big city. I cannot see you living here. You deserve the world. I cannot give you that."

There are too many "cannots" in that speech. I get his message loud and clear.

He pulls my hand toward him. "Come here."

I lean over him. Our lips find each other and become one.

Tears spill down on my face. Mixing with his own.

Instead of crying, why isn't he fighting for us? For me?

I promised myself I would not love harder than a man loves me again. I meant it.

I straighten up and put on my sunglasses.

As I walk out the door, I say, "Get better quickly. Those Cocoa Reef Resort guests need their cocktails."

Keston Kips closes his eyes. "Remember our Lucy. She's always in the sky."

I walk out of the hospital with my heart in a hundred pieces.

# Chapter Fifty-Four

April in New York is damp and chilly. Spring has barely sprung. Summer is a far-off thought.

I dive back into my old life, so I won't have time to think about Keston or St. Nicholas. And especially not about No Man's Land. I file away those memories and move on.

A lot has happened in the month I was gone.

Lisa's astrophysicist boyfriend asked her to marry him. The first social event I must attend is a bachelorette party. Because they've decided to marry in a month. Something about stars aligning.

Giselle comes to hang out at my condo before the party. We plan on taking an Uber to a restaurant near Columbia University where the party is being hosted by Lisa's graduate school astrophysicist friends.

"I bet they talk about string theory all night," Giselle laughs. "I'm just glad you're going. It's time you get out of the house."

"Why do people keep saying that? I go to work every day."

"But are you enjoying your work? Because you haven't spoken about your cases at all. Even before your island trip. And you used to."

"I'm not enjoying it," I confess. "But what choice do I have?"

She eyes me hard. I feel as if I'm in the principal's office being chastised.

"Anyway, going to a party or dinner or something fun is what I meant by getting out of the house." She swigs champagne from the bottle we bought for Lisa.

"Looks like we'll need to make a liquor stop on the way there. Per usual."

"I'm sorry." Giselle does not look at all sorry. It's part of our routine. She drinks while I dress. We started doing this in college. She's been my best friend for over twenty years.

I stop putting on my makeup.

"This may not be the right time. But I have to tell you something."

Giselle stops in mid-sip. "Yes?"

I sit next to her on the sofa. "It's hard."

She puts her glass on the coffee table and gives me all her attention.

"I have a daughter."

Giselle's face goes blank.

"Did you hear me?"

"Uh-huh. Can you explain, please?"

I relay the entire story. The way I told Keston. I don't leave out anything. When I'm done. Giselle wraps me in her arms. "Oh, sweetie. I'm so sorry you couldn't tell me back then."

Good thing I didn't put on all my makeup. Because we blubber over each other.

"Does anyone else know? Does your daughter know?" Giselle asks. Then in an excited voice, she adds, "Can I be her aunt?"

I laugh, relieved at how well she's taking it. After I hid it from her for so many years.

"Thank you for understanding."

Giselle, who never cries, being a principal of a middle school, sheds more tears. "I would have been by your side, you know. Through it all."

Now it's me who feels sorry for that twenty-one-year-old girl who didn't trust anyone to share her secret.

Look at what we miss out on if we don't open ourselves up. And pretend we're okay.

"How come you're telling me this now? Is it because you almost died on that island?"

"Keston suggested I should stop hiding my true self behind secrets."

"Wise man."

Yeah, he is."

"You need to tell me that story one day. I know it's too hard for you to talk about right now. But don't make me wait twenty years again."

<h1 style="text-align:center">Chapter Fifty-Five</h1>

The party is fun with women laughing, sharing love stories, playing games, cutting into a large cake, and chomping on penis popsicles, with a spa day as a prize for who can eat her penis the fastest.

I didn't think the astrophysicists had it in them. They pulled off a festive and sexy bachelorette party that Lisa loved.

And that I survived.

"How're you feeling?" Mikah asks as we watch Lisa squeal and holler while opening her bridal shower gifts.

Given the short time between her engagement and wedding, the bridal shower and bachelorette party are combined into one event.

"I feel fine."

"Liar."

"Leave CJ alone. She's been through hell." Katana, who looks like she'll have her baby any moment, rubs circles on my back. "We were so worried about you."

I drop my head on her shoulder. She's our Mother Hen.

Giselle squeezes my thigh. "CJ is stronger than you know."

"Thanks guys," I say.

"Are you and Marcus getting back together?" Mikah asks boldly.

"No. He's been calling but . . ."

"We like him now," Mikah adds. "If that makes a difference."

"Oh, you like him now."

Lisa shouts over the crowd. "Hey guys don't talk about anything important without me!"

Mikah swats her hand at Lisa. "Go back to your gifts. We'll give you the tea later."

To me she says, "He proved himself ten times over. When we got your SOS, we called him. He'd gotten your emergency signal and was on a plane within an hour."

"Less," Giselle says. "He dragged his private pilot out of bed. Physically. And had the emergency medical helicopter waiting on St. Nicholas for his arrival."

"Oh. I didn't know that."

"It was like Mark Darcy racing to rescue Bridget Jones when she got arrested overseas," Katana says dreamily.

I roll my eyes.

"What we mean is that Marcus must love you fiercely to do that," Giselle says.

"Fine. I'll have dinner with him. He's asked a few times."

"What are you waiting for? Did you fall out of love with him already?" Mikah stares at me with narrowed eyes. "Or did you meet someone else? Did you and the bartender bone during the whole fiasco?"

If they only knew.

"I said I'd have a meal with Marcus," I snap.

"She hated the bartender, remember? Too bad it was him you got stranded with," Lisa says, pulling up on the last bit of conversation.

"Can we please stop talking about it?" I press a hand to my heart.

Giselle wraps a protective arm around me. Mikah mouths, "I'm sorry."

Keeping another secret from my friends is not my intention. But if I'm never seeing Keston Kips again, what's the point of talking about him?

# Chapter Fifty-Six

One month later, after the slush is gone and the trees are green, Giselle suggests we rent a car and drive upstate to see my mother.

"You can't tell her you gave birth to a baby girl nineteen years ago over the phone. This is something that needs to be done in person."

I've been dreading having this conversation. I'm relieved Giselle is offering to act as a buffer for when I blurt out the news that I denied my mom her only grandchild.

On a beautiful day in May, Giselle and I end up crossing the Gov. Mario Cuomo Bridge, leaving New York City behind. The sun sparkles on the Hudson River.

The further north we travel, the more trees, streams, and wide-open spaces. Soon, we pass Bear Mountain, and fields of wildflowers.

"You're lucky you grew up here."

I don't say what I'm thinking. That all this nature reminds me of No Man's Land and Keston.

Music plays softly on the car's speakers. I drive as Giselle talks about her job, her students, and the upcoming graduation for her eighth graders. She's also desperately looking for a new place to live over the summer. To be closer to the school.

"I'll keep my eye out," I assure her.

"Great. Or else I'll be sleeping on your couch."

I laugh. "Like in college?"

"Exactly."

"I would love to be a principal of a school in one of these small cozy towns. But those jobs are non-existent. The principals here live and die in their jobs."

I laugh. "They do."

Most drivers bypass the exit to my small hometown unless they go to college there. Mom is a professor of English at the private liberal arts college, and my dad, before he moved away, was a teacher at the local high school in the Art Department.

Their relationship dwindled away over finances. Or lack of it. Dad was laid off and decided to try and make it as a full-time painter.

Mom's fear of living paycheck to paycheck as we did most of my life when she was a single mom is the reason she's gung-ho about Marcus. He represents everything she longed for growing up and in her adult life.

Security.

"I love these cute, small towns," Giselle says gleefully as we pass signs for the Spring Flower festival, with an ice cream eating contest and a swing dance tonight.

"Can we go to the festival?" she pleads.

"The last time I attended the Spring Flower festival was as a teenager before I left for Howard."

"Why?"

"My mom."

"Oh, yeah."

"I was afraid I'd blurt out the news. I'm forty years old and still afraid to tell my mom."

Giselle rubs my shoulder. "It's a difficult topic no matter your age."

At noon, we arrive outside the front door of my childhood home. It's a small Tudor house with slanted roofs, a pretty rose-filled garden, an arched red door, and a lion's head knocker.

Giselle squeals. "It looks like something from Snow White."

"It's an English professor's home. Think Jane Austen."

"You ready?" Giselle asks.

"Game on."

Giselle fists bumps me.

I'd told Mom we'd get here around noon, so she's not surprised to see us.

"Lordy, honey." She envelops me in a big hug. "The grandfather clock can stop ticking. The prodigal daughter has returned."

"Haha, Mom. Very funny."

Mom met Giselle at our college graduation. But it's been many years since they've seen each other.

Giselle and Mom hit it off immediately. Mom gives her a

tour of the house while I go on the back porch and out into the garden. The giant oak tree was my friend growing up.

No wonder I connected with Prince Harry so deeply. I have an affinity for trees.

When we're all seated outside, Mom brings out a tray with her homemade lemonade and a charcuterie board.

"You've moved on from scones and cucumber sandwiches?" I ask.

To Giselle, I say, "Mom is the only Black woman who served cucumber sandwiches."

Mom goes back to the kitchen and returns with a platter of the infamous sandwiches.

"Never mind," I tell Giselle. "Some things never go out of style."

Mom sits and folds one crisp blue jean-clad leg over the other. "We had our fair share of tea parties in this garden," she smiles. "Glad you remember."

I lean back, my heart pounding. I eye the green leaves rustling above my head. The trellis of roses along the fence. "How's Ginger?"

"She died."

"Ginger was our neighbor's cat who drove Mom crazy climbing over the fence and peeing all over her garden."

"She ate the roses."

"Poor Ginger."

After we've eaten and chatted about my job, Giselle's desire to work upstate, and Mom's summer teaching schedule, a hush descends.

Ironically, silences of anticipation are called *pregnant* pauses. Giselle's eyes urge me to speak up.

"Mom, I have something I must tell you. I should have told you a long time ago."

"What is it, Carmela Anne?"

She's in professor mode. Using my full first name.

Giselle pats my knee. Mom raises her perfectly groomed eyebrows, her gaze focused on Giselle's hand.

She gives me a withering look. "I'm an ally. If you're trying to tell me you're gay, I am fully supportive."

Giselle snatches her hand from my knee. "No, Mrs. Jones. That's not it."

I stifle a nervous laugh. "I wish it was that."

"Oh, then what?" Her eyes light up. "Are you and Marcus . . . *getting engaged*? Is that it?"

"No, Mom. We're dating. Casually."

She scoffs. "How can you casually date a man you've been with for five years?"

A question I ask myself regularly. But it's true. Right after Lisa's bachelorette party, I followed up on my promise to the girls and started dating him again.

I had to swallow the terrible pill that Keston was right. He and I were two different people. Living two separate lives.

The stranded on a desert island business is something I must chalk up to one of life's crazy happenings. Strangely, Marcus has stepped up and revealed a softer, caring side.

He's more attentive. Planning great dates like concerts, special museum viewings, and the best restaurants. As if he thinks I need big city culture to forget my small island adventure.

Mom clears her throat. "There's time for you and Marcus to figure things out. What is it then?"

# Chapter Fifty-Seven

My mother worked hard to make sure I had great opportunities in life. She takes great pride in her reputation, and in mine, as an extension of hers. Getting pregnant when I was barely out of my teenage years is not a statistic she'd have accepted. She might have disowned me.

*Am I too old to be disowned now?*

I sit forward, look her right in the eye. My heart hammers in anticipation of the disappointment or anger I'll see there.

"When I was a junior in college, I got pregnant."

Mom's brown face drains of color. "You what?"

I pray for tears not to fall. I hear Keston's sing-song voice telling me how amazing I am. I square my shoulders and find the courage that I lacked twenty years ago.

"I was scared to tell you, Mom. I was afraid to tell anyone."

Mom stares at me like she doesn't know me. I swallow and continue.

"I didn't even tell my best friend. I couldn't face everyone's disappointment in me."

"What did you do?" Her voice is cold as steel.

"I had a daughter. Her birthday is August 2nd. I gave her up for adoption. It was with a wonderful agency who found her a loving family."

I've never seen my mother cry. She reels back, as if I slapped her, eyes brimming with tears.

For a second, I almost say I'm kidding.

"How could you?" she rasps out. "No wonder you didn't come home that summer. Or any summer after that. You were too ashamed to face me. You've given away our flesh and blood to strangers. Strangers!" she cries.

Giselle grips my knee. I feel as if Mom sucker punched me.

"I know," I sob. "I thought you'd hate me. I couldn't raise a child at that time. I did what I felt was best for the baby."

"What was best was for you to come to me."

Mom drops her head in her hands. "How did this happen?"

The relief I feel from telling my secret is overshadowed by the guilt from the pain I'm causing. Were some secrets meant to go to your grave with you?

"I'm so sorry, Mom. The girl I was back then did the best she could. I'm not that person anymore."

I rely on Keston's words. They hit hard when he said them on the island, and now I know they're true.

"I've learned that who we are changes over time. Our experiences are how we grow and learn to make better choices. It's called living with your mistakes. That's what I'm doing, Mom. I'm living with it and trying to do better."

Mom raises her tear-streaked face. "What's her name? Where is she?"

Giselle speaks because I'm choking up too much.

"We don't know that information. But CJ filled out forms years ago to let the agency know to contact her if her daughter wants to meet her."

Mom looks at me with the warrior eyes she saves for anyone who dares to cross her. "Put down my name and contact information immediately. She's nineteen. She may want to contact her grandmother instead."

I nod numbly. "I'll do that. I'm sorry. It was a chaotic time for me. I wasn't thinking properly."

"You sure weren't," Mom says, anger in her voice now. She wipes her eyes. "Why do I feel like I'm to blame for you being afraid to tell me? Was I too tough on you? All I wanted was for you to be a strong person."

I recall the big tree lying across Keston. The strength I needed to carry him out from under it. The horrible mud I raked through with my bare hands.

"You're not to blame. It was I who acted cowardly. I have something else to tell you, Mom. You too, Giselle."

We spend the rest of the day sitting under the oak tree. I relay to my mother and my best friend the story of No Man's Land.

The shock of discovering we were stranded, fishing with my beach dress, eating coconuts, bananas, and breadfruit right off the tree.

Mom and Giselle laugh at the image I paint of me fishing, hiking barefoot, and sleeping on palm fronds.

They gasp in horror at my almost dying from heatstroke. When I talk about Keston running through the rainforest with me in his arms to the waterfall and dumping me in the cool water, they exchange glances.

The day of the hurricane is difficult to talk about. When my mind goes to that almost fatal day, I start to shake.

The slightest sound of thunder paralyzes me. Lightning brings pure terror.

I haven't spoken about the fear of being outside with strong winds or rain to anyone. But I want to tell my mother now. She deserves to know she raised a strong daughter. She raised a survivor.

My voice trembles as I describe the last full day Keston and I spent on the island.

I recount how the giant tree crashed down in the forest causing Keston to push me out of the way as he took the full force of the blow.

Mom grabs my hands. Her eyes frantic, racing up and down my body as if looking for broken limbs.

"Go on." She doesn't let go of my hands. Giselle sits like a statue in her chair. She knew it was a scary time for me, but this is the first she's hearing about the actual events.

I sob about how Keston's scream of pain echoed in the forest, louder than the thunder.

"It was awful. I didn't know what to do. There was so much thunder, lightning, rain, and we were in the dark. I couldn't see a thing."

Mom hands me a glass of water from the pitcher she'd brought out earlier. I gulp it down. "You don't have to say anymore."

"No, I want to tell you."

I describe digging in the mud, being a human excavator, to get Keston out from under the tree. "There was blood. And broken bones. I was so scared."

Mom and Giselle sit frozen in their seats.

"I made a splint. Tied it to his leg with strips of my crocheted dress."

"That dress is the hero of this story," Giselle says softly, shaking her head.

"You dug in the dirt? With your bare hands?" Mom's eyes widen with shock. "You're terrified of gardening."

I laugh demonically. "I still am. That was a once-in-a-lifetime event."

"It sounds like a Netflix movie," Giselle remarks. "What happened next?"

"The rest is fuzzy in my head. I half carried him to a silk cotton tree. Keston had told me to run and hide there when the tree fell on him. Because other stuff was crashing down in the forest."

"But you stayed. And rescued him," my mom says admiringly. "I'm so proud of you, sweetheart."

Her words fill my heart. For years I've felt as if I didn't deserve her praise. Which somehow translated into me thinking less of myself.

"Thank you, Mom." I wipe my eyes. It doesn't matter how old or young I am, nothing can replace my mother's praise.

"Go on, CJ, I'm dying to hear the rest." Giselle perches on the edge of her chair.

"After getting Keston inside the tree, which looks like someplace Winnie the Pooh would live, I sat up and made SOS calls and prayed a lot."

"When did Marcus arrive?" Giselle asks.

I fill them in on how the next morning, I raced through the

forest to the beach because I'd heard a weed wacker. Which turned out to be a helicopter.

Mom and Giselle roll their eyes.

"And I dropped lavender petals to mark the path back to Keston."

Mom gasps, "Did it work?"

Giselle shakes her head, "So smart. You need to teach a survivor course at the Y."

"I was smart, wasn't I?" I beam. "It totally worked."

"What happened when you saw Marcus jump out of the helicopter?" Mom asks.

"Did you run into his arms?" asks Giselle. "Did he race across the sand and hug you?"

"No. I was a mess. When they landed, I was naked, covered in sand, mud, and ash. And desperate to rescue Keston. There was no hugging."

"Keston would have hugged you first."

I eye my mother. "What?"

Giselle nods. "I agree. Keston would have hugged you immediately."

"I hadn't thought about it. But you're right. He's a protector."

"Of you," my mother clarifies. "He protects *you*."

It feels good to talk about Keston. To share my trauma with people who love me. But also, to remind myself I saved him, just as much as he saved me.

"I only have one question," my mother says when I finish my tale.

"What?" I pop a warm cucumber sandwich into my mouth. Ugh!

"Why aren't you with Keston Kips right now?"

# Chapter Fifty-Eight

Mom's question comes up all summer. No matter how I explain to her and Giselle that Keston and I have accepted we are total opposites, with different lives and nothing in common, they don't see it that way.

Giselle thinks I'm in denial and should call him.

Mom says I need time to process the trauma. "But don't mistake the forest for the trees."

"Meaning what?" I asked the Professor of English Literature who likes to reference ancient proverbs.

"While you focus on the details of your differences, you may miss the bigger picture."

When I looked at her blankly, she sighed deeply. "You *love* him. He *loves* you. That's the bigger picture."

It's shocking that my mom is now Team Keston after all those years of being Team Marcus. She says she never cared about Marcus's money. She just wants me to find a protector. Who loves me. And Keston is all that and more.

She has no idea the "more" is out of this world. For obvious reasons, I left out the spicy parts of our misadventure.

Mom champions Keston for restarting my relationship with her. Since telling her my secret, I have visited almost every weekend over the summer.

We hit up the town's festivals and attend her summer college faculty events together.

I have time because I've handed off my casework to senior associates at the firm and I'm focused on signing new clients.

It's crazy how many people contact me every week to represent them after my and Keston's survival story went viral around the globe.

I don't know who started it. Could have been one of the paramedics who documented the rescue with photos and videos.

All I know is I'm reaping big benefits from my "heroic" deeds.

CEOs of cruise ships, theme parks, and airlines love the idea of a survivor of a desert island hurricane representing them in court. It means the jury already has compassion for me. It also means I have time to step away from the office on weekends to catch up with Mom.

Mom is thrilled to have me back in my old bedroom. Giselle comes along most weekends. She's met a handsome, rugged vineyard owner named Hank and hangs out with him.

He's the same age as Keston and teases her that he's always had a thing for older women.

Am I a bit jealous my best friend found love with a hot younger man while I'm struggling with my feelings for Marcus? Yes!

But I'm happy for her too. She says if it weren't for me, she'd never have met Hank.

As for Marcus, I see him during the week when he's in town. He dazzles me with fantastic dates that require me to dress up in ball gowns and accompany him in his knockout tuxedos.

The paparazzi snap our photos which appear in gossip magazines and newspaper columns with headlines like, *Is Marriage in the Cards for Billionaire Marcus O'Brien and Lawyer Carmela Jones?*

Of course, it's all lies. I'm not getting engaged right now even if he asked.

"What about you?" I ask Mom one evening in late August as we sit in the garden sipping wine. We spent the day blueberry picking with Giselle and Hank.

"There's got to be some silver foxes up here for you to fall in love with."

She scoffs and changes the subject. "Any news from Keston?"

I cut my throat with a pretend knife. "Mom, that's not going to happen. Please accept it."

"I will when you accept it."

"What do you mean?" I sip the chilled Pinot Gris we got from Hank earlier, tapping my finger on the glass stem as I wait for her to tell me what I already know.

That I'm not that into Marcus anymore because I'm hung up on Keston Kips. Truth is I can't stop thinking about him. I'd be on the metro, in yoga class, or at my desk and I'd close my eyes and see Keston.

His smile is imprinted on my heart. His lips and tongue are as bold in my daydreams as they were in real life on that rock.

Shirtless, rugged, brown eyes laughing at me as I struggle to braid a palm leaf mat.

But we have no future so why torture ourselves with a long-distance relationship? I'd end up resenting him for not wanting to move to the city. He'd hate me if he did.

Before Mom can give me a speech about following my heart, her phone rings. She holds up a slim finger. "One sec."

A glance at her phone screen brings a frown to her smooth features. I'm privy to the one-sided conversation.

"Hello?"

"Yes, this is she."

You know those transformations on people's faces when they find out they've won the lottery? Or when Oprah brings out their beloved teacher from fifth grade who helped them become who they are today? That's the look that comes over Mom's face.

I immediately know who's calling.

I want to scream, "Give me the phone."

I leap up and circle Mom like a shark as she speaks quietly.

*Hurry up, let me speak to her.*

"Yes, she is the same Carmela Anne Jones who was stranded on a deserted island during a hurricane."

"Yes, the same one." Mom stands up and pushes me away with one arm.

"It's true. She dug a man free with her bare hands and saved his life."

*Thump thump thump.* My poor heart.

"She's right here. We were having a glass of wine together."

Long pause.

"I am your grandmother. No, I don't mind. You can call me anything you'd like. What's your name?" Mom's free hand twists her necklace beads around and around.

Tears flow down my face with no stopping in sight.

It doesn't matter if she doesn't want to talk to me, I tell myself. *She found me!*

"Lucy Pennell. That's a lovely name."

My mouth drops open.

*Lucy?* Her name is *Lucy?*

My first thought is that I must tell Keston.

The last thing he said to me was to keep looking for our Lucy. Now it appears that she found me because of him.

That's the first thought I have.

The second is that Mom was right all along.

Love is the big picture. The trees are important, but who you go into the forest with is what matters. I'd choose Keston any day.

Mom and Lucy—*my Lucy*—speak for a few more minutes before hanging up.

Raw emotions flash across my mother's face. Wonder, sadness, delight, and back to wonder.

When she hangs up, she shouts, "Yes!" My steadfast, no-

nonsense mother does some version of the dance called the *bump* against my hip.

"That was Lucy."

I've prepared myself for the fact that she may not want to meet me.

"She's at college in North Carolina. She found out about you last year when she turned eighteen."

"She's known about me?"

Mom nods. "She read about your exploits on No Man's Land."

"They weren't *exploits*," I murmur.

"She said you sound awesome."

"She did?"

Mom's head bobs like a dashboard doggie's. "She wants to meet you. But she's afraid. Her words were, 'I hope I could be that brave one day.'"

My hands clasp my heart. "What did you tell her?"

"I told her she'd already done the bravest thing by calling."

I look at my mother and my heart melts. "That was the perfect thing to say."

"I know."

"Did she say when?"

"It's not definite. She wants to check with her parents. Sounds like they're very supportive. But she's thinking of coming over the Thanksgiving holiday."

"That would be perfect."

"Figure out your life, missy. Because your firstborn is arriving to meet us."

I scream and jump up and down like a teenager.

"You're giving me a headache," Mom grouses. But the smile on her face is wider than the trees in the forest.

# Chapter Fifty-Nine

Keston Kips and I belong together. I can't believe it's taken me this long to figure it out.

Maybe I was waiting to find my daughter to feel complete enough to accept his love. Maybe I needed time to process the traumatic events as Mom said.

But I'm ready.

He can't come up here. So, I'll go down there. It's not the details that matter, it's our love.

Except before I leave, I need to tell Marcus it is officially over. I think he knows. I haven't wanted to restart the physical side of our relationship even after months of dating. No man could think we have anything more than a casual dating friendship.

Marcus and I meet at the bar downstairs from my job. It's packed with lawyers, so we find a quiet booth and slide in on either side.

He orders a bottle of wine even though he hardly drinks alcohol. I read the menu although I know every item on it.

My hands pat the table nervously. Where's adrenaline when you need it?

"How's work going?" he asks.

"Fine." *Tap tap tap tap.*

His hand presses on top of mine. "Carmela . . ."

"Marcus."

"You haven't been yourself. It's been months since you came back from the Cocoa Reef Resort. I've been patient. Showing you that I love you."

He stops at my sharp intake of breath. In my mind's eye, I see him jumping out of the helicopter. It's difficult to break up with someone who'd fly to a deserted island to find you.

"Why do you love me?"

He looks at the expensive watch on his wrist. "Sorry. I have a conference call. But this is more important."

"Why do you love me?" Maybe if I could understand that, I'd feel a deeper connection to him. Even with all the fun dates, the emotional intimacy, so easy with Keston, is missing with Marcus.

He rubs his chin. "That's easy."

I smile hesitantly. "Really?" Maybe I was wrong. Maybe he does love me enough to want to make a real commitment.

"You're strong and beautiful. You're uncomplicated."

I hold up a hand. "Uncomplicated?"

Ha! Keston would beg to differ. "Any other reason?"

"You don't complain. You don't ask me to do ridiculous things like call and text you regularly. You're not clingy or needy. You're perfect."

"What about how I want to settle down, get married, move out of the city, have children and a big backyard."

The lines on his forehead deepen. "You never said that."

I shake my head. "I know. I'm sorry. I didn't ask for much from you. I didn't want to burden you."

"Exactly why I love you."

"Marcus, you can get a pet to be all those things you love. Well, maybe a cat. A dog may be clingy and needy. The point is you don't love me. You don't even know me. I *am* complicated. I *am* clingy to the right man. I *want* sex every day, if possible, but I'll take twice a week. I want to make love outdoors and scream at the top of my lungs."

"Hush, Carmela, you're making a scene."

"I don't care."

"You've changed more than I thought."

"And it's about time. If we don't change, we die."

He grabs his wine glass and downs it. "What are you saying?"

"That it's over. You don't really love me. But I want you to find the right person for you. Everyone deserves their person."

His lips flatten. "Not this again. You're breaking up with me for no reason. Where are you going to find a guy like me? At forty? Who lets you live your life, work at your firm, hang out with your girlfriends as much as you want, and doesn't ask too much of you?"

I stand. Slip my bag over my shoulder.

"Thanks for the wine. Thanks for rescuing me and Keston from that island. Thanks for the medical care to save his leg. But you know what Marcus, I'll let you go now. I'll *let* you find someone else. I'll *let* you go take your conference calls. I'm headed to St. Nicholas."

I stride to the door.

He stands up. "Carmela Jones . . ."

I turn around. "It's CJ. It's *always* been CJ. You can't even get my name right."

"Did that island bartender call you?" The bitterness in his tone stops me.

"Why do you ask?"

His eyes turn steely. "We made a deal. I want to know if he's going back on it."

I walk slowly, carefully toward Marcus. My voice is soft and precise. "What. Kind. Of. Deal?"

"I would pay for the best medical care to save his leg if he never called you again." His voice does not waver.

I'm so shocked at his proud admission that I'm at a loss for words. I stare at Marcus with growing disgust. He thought he could *pay* for me?

"So did he call you?" he asks.

"It was Keston's leg for my love? No . . . my *complacency*?" I finally see what my girlfriends saw long before me. Marcus is ruthless in every area of his life, not just business.

Blood rushes to my head. I want to pick up the bottle of wine and throw it at him.

"I bet you didn't know he gave you up so easily."

He thinks he has a weapon to hurt me with.

Marcus doesn't know me at all. The angrier I get, the calmer I feel.

If there's anything I learned it's that I may moan about

needing a/c, run from scary bats, and don't get me started on creepy crawlies, but when big stuff happens, I shut up and show up.

"I'm glad he took that deal," I smile sweetly. "He'd be stupid not to take it. Lose his leg? That's a no-brainer."

I've spent a lot of time negotiating settlement agreements for clients. The number one rule is to never put all your cards on the table. Don't let the other side know your weakness.

My weakness right now is anger at myself for deserting Keston when he needed me. I should have contacted him. Giselle and my mother were right.

But I didn't call him because I was holding on to the stupid notion that he had to prove he loved me first before I'd reveal my true feelings. I let pride lead the way.

But isn't love supposed to be a two-way street?

Aren't you both supposed to show up for each other, and it doesn't matter who says what first?

Marcus frowns as if he can hear my thoughts.

"He's a bartender. On a remote island. With nothing to offer you."

I cluck my tongue. "Then why do you feel so threatened by him?"

Oh Lordy, I did it again. I let pride lead. I should have thanked Marcus and said goodbye.

Nicely.

If there's a rule of thumb to follow, it's *don't piss off a billionaire.*

The taxi motors up the twisting driveway lined with hibiscus bushes and coconut trees to reach the open-air reception plaza of the Cocoa Reef Resort. The marble floors and gilt mirrors gleam even more than they did the last time I checked in. Probably spruced up after the hurricane.

I booked a Deluxe Room instead of the villa, but the G.M. comes out personally to greet me.

"We put you in another exquisite villa. To apologize for the fiasco that occurred the last time you stayed with us. Anything you need, please let me know. How long will you be staying?"

"I'm not sure."

"Doesn't matter. The villa is yours. We'd like your stay to be relaxing and uneventful."

"Thank you," I shake his hand. Meanwhile, my heart hopscotches about in my chest. "I hope it's not *too* uneventful."

The manager departs with a chuckle. The concierge approaches with the welcome rum punch.

My hand trembles as I take a sip. I'm getting closer to Keston by the second. Am I ready to face him?

It's a tad too sugary. I swallow my taste with disappointment. It's not a KK special.

"Do you have a new bartender?" I ask the concierge.

She blinks. "Dex has been with us for a while. He got promoted recently. Is anything wrong with the drink?"

"No," I assure her. "It's fine."

I decide to hold off on interrogating the poor woman and jump in the golf cart waiting to take me to my luxury villa.

A lot can happen in six months. Keston may have a girlfriend. He may have left the island, though I doubt that. He may not work here anymore. He may not want to see me again after I walked away from him while he was in the hospital. I hope he'll understand I was confused and traumatized. Unsure about what I felt.

I had imagined our reunion as a romantic scenario. I'd walk into the resort's beach bar, surprise Keston by throwing my arms around him, and declare my love. He'd be overjoyed to see me and sweep me off my feet with love and adoration in his eyes.

But nothing on St. Nicholas goes according to plan. I'll have to regroup.

"You're back!" Dex greets me with open arms. "How are you? You look beautiful."

I blush to the tips of my curly hair. This twenty-something young man is so genuine and open-hearted.

"Thank you. Congratulations on being promoted to head bartender."

He ducks his head with the shyest grin. "It's temporary. Until Keston returns."

"Oh, when is he returning?" I ask in what is hopefully a non-groupie manner.

"That's what everyone wants to know. He had some setbacks with physical therapy."

"Setbacks?" I clutch my throat.

Dex nods. "A lot of pain. Another surgery two months ago. I think he's on the mend now. I went to see him last week."

My ears perk up. "You saw him at home? Where does he live?"

Dex crushes ice with his blender for a cocktail in progress. After he's delivered the drink to the guest, he leans on the bar and says, "He doesn't want visitors. I only went to drop off his check. The resort is paying to keep him on staff and help with his disability."

I sit back on my stool. The only reason Keston wouldn't want visitors is if he's in a lot of pain. Flashbacks of the bone sticking out of his leg make me shudder.

I should have stayed to help.

"He told you he doesn't want visitors?"

Dex nods.

"People were showing up with bottles of alcohol to cheer him up and he started drinking a lot. He's gone cold turkey. Doesn't want to see alcohol. And since everyone on the island drinks, he's banned them all until he recovers."

"Harsh."

"But necessary."

"Do you think he'd want to see me?" I hold my breath waiting for the answer.

Dex shrugs. "Only one way to find out."

Turns out Keston's home is *way* down the beach. I wade across the river I'd once enjoyed on the resort grounds. Hustle through a small but dense forest I would have avoided in the past. It's a piece of cake now.

I hike over a hill following a track with bamboo and tall grasses on either side. It's inhabited by cows and goats.

Dex didn't say anything about animals. He did tell me I could take a taxi in the morning.

I didn't want to wait. I asked him to point me in the right direction down the beach.

"Just follow the tracks. You can't miss it."

Island speak for it's a long, *long* way away.

After forty minutes of trekking, I arrive at the edge of a golden sand beach.

I'm soggy with sweat. My dress and sandals need a good washing.

I take in the simple wooden house set back from the water.

Lights illuminate the curtains fluttering at the windows. A delicious smell emanates from inside.

Keston's home, though small and very modest, enjoys a stunning view of the sunset.

I don't know if I'm mad that I waited so long to come, or jealous of his epic beach-front property.

I rearrange my clothes, dust off leaves, and touch up my lips with a lip gloss in a sunset pink glow.

Great. I'm ready for whatever.

As I get ready to step out from the shadows and announce myself, a tall man walks out of the wooden house. He has a slight limp. He takes a seat and places his legs up on the porch railing. The curly hair is unmistakable.

Keston Kips picks up a guitar and strums some bars, singing a melancholy song of love and loss as night descends in Caribbean fashion, setting off the scent of jasmine flowers in the air.

# Chapter Sixty-One

My breath hitches. My feet refuse to move forward. I'm afraid to speak and break this spell of enchantment. After years of searching for Mr. Right, here he is in front of me. He's nowhere near perfect. But neither am I.

The moon is a curved crescent in the darkening sky. Stars

brighten the universe as my heart fills with love watching the man whose spirit has knitted itself onto my soul for eternity.

Without realizing, I've inched closer and closer to the porch. Toward Keston's deep voice as he sings about waiting for his love to return.

Suddenly, Keston stops playing the guitar. He stands and takes the three front steps down to the sand.

"Hello?"

He looks up at the sky. I do, too.

"CJ? Nah, that's dumb."

I take a tiny step. "It's me," I whisper.

"CJ?" his voice is strained. "Am I losing my mind?"

"No. It's me." I hurry to walk out of the shadows.

It's a moment I imagined a hundred times. Keston Kips and I are face to face again.

Parents say the first time they see their child, they feel a deep, unbreakable bond that goes beyond any feeling they've ever experienced before. It's as if love is finally explained.

That's how I feel. Looking into Keston Kips' dark eyes, my heart ascends to a place in the galaxy, next to the stars and the moon. Because nothing on earth can express how I feel.

Keston reaches my side and picks me up without saying a word.

"Your leg . . . ," I protest.

"Is much better."

I don't argue with him. He carries me as if I am a precious jewel right up the steps to the porch, sitting down on the rustic porch swing with me still on his lap. His arms are steel around my body like he's never going to let me go.

"I love the porch swing," I say dumbly. "Did you make it yourself? I didn't know you played the guitar. Or sang?"

My mind is a butterfly flitting here, there, and everywhere.

"You came back."

That's all he says before his mouth finds mine. He crushes my lips with a kiss so forceful and possessive, sucking the air out of me, leaving me breathless and spent, that I know without a doubt he is sealing our fates with this kiss.

"You came back," he says, raising his head, holding me at arm's length as if to make sure it's really me.

"I did."

"For how long?" he frowns then shakes his head. "Doesn't matter. You're here now."

His legs look as strong as before. His arms even more so. Like he's been working out a lot.

"You look great, honey." Words choke up inside me remembering the last time I saw him with his leg up in traction. I run my hands up and down his arms. I slide them along his muscled thighs. "Better than great."

"It was hard work. But I'm almost there. I'm running on the beach every day to help with the limp."

"I'm sorry I left you." I sob out. "I can't believe I left you and went away."

He presses my head to his chest. "Hush, baby. You couldn't stay here. St. Nicholas was recovering from a hurricane. You suffered a lot, too. Mentally, emotionally. It was traumatic as hell. I was worried about you. But, I'd promised . . ." He stops.

"I know about Marcus's blackmail. I'm glad you let him help you fix your leg."

"I'm paying him back. Slowly but surely. As soon as I paid him, I was coming to get you."

"Really?"

He nods, his eyes serious and sad. "I missed you so much. The pain of not knowing how you were doing was worse than the pain in my leg. How are you anyway? Why *did* you return? I hope it's to be with me because I'm not letting you go."

I laugh happily. "I'm not going anywhere. I want to stay for as long as I can. Until at least Thanksgiving."

"When the hell is that?"

"End of November."

He sighs in relief. "Thank goodness. I have time to kidnap you."

"Want to know why I have to go then?"

"Not really. I don't want to think about it."

"My daughter found me," I say, in a hushed tone.

Keston's eyes light up like twinkly lights on a Christmas tree. "That is wonderful news, CJ. What is she like?"

"I'll meet her at Thanksgiving. I wish you could come."

"Me too. Maybe I can."

I beam. "The best part, Kes, is her name is Lucy."

He shakes his head. "I don't believe you."

"It's true," I grin. "Her name is Lucy."

His eyes shine with unshed tears. "She's your Lucy in the sky with diamonds."

"She is."

"Just like you are mine."

"I am."

"Okay, Thanksgiving it is. But then we come right back. And invite her to come too."

"Seriously, you'll probably get tired of me soon. My friends say I complain a lot. I'm bitchy and . . ."

He nips my lips with his teeth. "Don't talk about my baby like that. You are wonderful. A little high maintenance, but nothing I can't handle. I never want to *not* be around you. I've been tortured long enough."

"You really mean all that?" I ask.

"You are perfect for me. I have no doubt. My heart knows what it wants. And it wants you, Carmela Anne Jones. CJ.

Come what may. Distance, age, professions, temperaments. You're a pain in the ass, but I love you. All of you. Forever."

I press my lips together, so I don't cry like a big baby before I say my piece.

"I love you too. I knew for sure when I saw you out here under the moon. My heart and soul felt at peace. Because you're my home."

Keston kisses me deeply, arms gripping me like he never wants to let me go. The moon shines its crescent light upon us in approval.

"Remember the night we met?" he asks, a twinkle in his eyes.

"Definitely not a meet-cute to write home about."

"But it was for me. Because I fell in love with you the first night after you blurted out your sorrows about your ex-boyfriend. I could tell you were a woman who loved deeply. And I wanted that kind of love."

"I was mad you pretended to be a therapist."

"I had to do everything to try and make it right. You had me acting crazy. Walking on the hot beach to carry a special drink to you. The next day I whipped up a breakfast smoothie and waited for you to show up. I've never done that for any hotel guests. Then when you jumped on the boat cruise, I followed you. I wasn't thinking. I just hopped on."

I stare at him in wonder. "You did all that for me?"

"Woman, you had me in my feelings from day one. It was always you."

I gaze at him under lowered eyelids. "It will always be you for me, too."

# Chapter Sixty-Two

Keston and I talk all night. We walk on the sand so we can stretch out our legs. We sit on the front steps of his beach house eating enamel bowls full of crab and dumpling stew he made earlier. From crabs he'd caught on the rocks in front of his house.

"Can I get this recipe?" I lick my bowl and spoon clean.

"Stay tuned. Tomorrow is iguana night in the Kips household."

I groan and push him. "No way."

Dawn finds us snuggling on the porch swing, two peas in a pod.

"It's time to go to bed, CJ. Come on."

Keston picks up my sleepy body in his arms. He kicks the door shut behind us.

I didn't know what to expect, but his bedroom is simple and clean. White-washed walls, a yellow chenille bedspread, and an air conditioning that pumps lovely cold air around us.

"Ahh!" I stretch out, arms above my head, toes pointed. "This is heaven."

He flops down next to me. "Not yet."

"What you got there?" I glimpse a bag in his hand.

"My dry bag from No Man's Land."

I stare at it. "Why?"

He pulls out a silvery square and waves it in the air.

I squint. "Is that . . . ?" I can't finish my question.

"I saved it for you."

"You never used it?"

"I haven't been with anyone since. Haven't wanted to be with anyone."

"You're losing your player vibes, dude."

He lays a heavy arm across my raised arms trapping them there. "You have a choice."

"Yes?" I ask, my voice husky with longing.

He throws a large, muscled leg over my hips. I'm totally trapped now. He traces circles on my stomach. Feathers his fingers back and forth over my inner thigh.

Fire shoots up my spine. My back arches all by itself.

He draws circles around my belly button with one finger.

"We can do a repeat performance of your waterfall orgasms first . . ."

"Yeah?" I close my eyes as his tongue torments my nipples. One then the other, slowly circling them with the heat of his mouth.

My thighs tremble. That earth-shattering orgasm where I came so hard in his mouth? That is what he's asking me if I want.

"Yes, please."

"Or we can pick up where we left off that day."

He drops his thick heavy cock on my leg. A gift.

"Option two," I breathe unable to stop my cream from pooling between my thighs.

"I want to feel you inside me."

His steel is sheathed in the condom that was meant for us. But the heat from his cock burns me like a fiery sword.

"Look at me, baby. I want to see your eyes."

I stare up at him as his fingers gently push aside my folds. His sweet cock enters me, stretches, and hurts me. I cry out at the depth of it. The width of it. The fullness I feel. It's been so long. I feel tighter than I've ever been.

He groans loudly as his cock sinks inside my warmth. His hips rock against mine. I raise my hips to meet his, taking more of his shaft deep within.

His hand reaches between my legs. He knows my body's rhythm. He rocks his hips against mine, as his fingers stroke my aching clit.

"That's it," I cry. "That's it."

He grunts with pleasure.

"I've waited so long for this," he says, pumping hard.

My rhythm amps up to match his. We're soaring.

He throws my legs over his shoulders.

His rod penetrates deeper.

His eyes lock on mine.

"Come with me. It's too fucking good to stop," he swears.

I can't speak. My pussy is in agony. He thumbs my clit while stroking my inner goddess. My juices spill around us like a waterfall.

"You gonna come for me, baby."

"Yes," I say weakly.

With that, he thrusts deeply, leans forward, and rocks my clit with his hips. Over and over and over until I see stars in the back of my head.

"Oh my God!" I shout.

"Scream, baby."

"Yes!"

The headboard hits the wall hard. His body stiffens. His cock throbs inside my pussy walls. Pumping a boatload of come into the condom.

As he comes, he tongues my nipples while pressing on my clit. His still-hard cock doesn't stop.

It's the trinity of pleasures.

Stars disintegrate behind my eyelids.

"Don't stop," I beg.

"Never," he growls.

"Come again for me. As loud as you can."

I do as he asks again. I scream as if I've lost all my senses. This is what I've been missing. This is what I need.

The sweet ride goes on and on. My shouts of pleasure drown out the waves and everything else in the night.

As my body adjusts back to reality, I whisper, "That was . . ."

I have no words to describe it.

"I'm here for you, baby. Always and forever. I promise."

I fall into a dreamless sleep, wrapped in Keston's arms. I don't know what tomorrow will bring for us, but together we'll be ready for anything.

Dear Reader,
Please <u>Leave a Review</u> on Amazon to help others find this book! It can be as short as you want! It would mean a lot to me (and to CJ and Keston!). Thank you!
Lynn

Grab your exclusive bonus chapter about CJ and Keston's spicy relationship in the *Lime to My Coconut* here—>
https://BookHip.com/KZZXNXW
I promise you'll LOVE 🩶 it.

Lynn Joseph is from Trinidad & Tobago. When she's not writing her international romances, she can be found on a beach somewhere in the world. Or binge-watching *Hart of Dixie* and *The Vampire Diaries* over and over. Lynn lives in charming South Portland, Maine, and on the Caribbean Island of Tobago, where she's known as the Mermaid Queen. Join her on her journey of love, food, and romantic destinations (not necessarily in that order). www.lynnjosephbooks.com

# Stay Connected

Sign up for Lynn's newsletter and receive a FREE ebook, *Princess Aboard.* Plus be in the know for all the behind the scenes goodies and more!

Sign Up Here —>
https://BookHip.com/NKSQGRS

Follow her on social media:

Facebook -http://facebook.com/lynnjosephauthor
Instagram - https://www.instagram.com/lynnjosephbooks/
Bookbub - https://bit.ly/3Phcsuu
Amazon - https://amzn.to/3VTd8Kb
Goodreads -https://bit.ly/4gUtZo4

Lynn loves to hear from her readers and invites them to email her, anytime at lynn@lynnjosephbooks.com

www.lynnjosephbooks.com

# Also by Lynn Joseph

The Walker Sisters Forever Series

(Sweet Romance)

Gelato Forever

Olives Forever

Sangria Forever

Paris Forever

Christmas Forever

Cocoa Reef Resort Series

(Steamy Romance)

Lime to My Coconut

Rum to the Reggae

Spice for My Santa

Bubbly for

Princess Abroad

(Read for FREE! —> https://BookHip.com/NKSQGRS )

www.ingramcontent.com/pod-product-compliance
Lightning Source LLC
Chambersburg PA
CBHW032352310726
48973CB00007B/1981